SIGNIFICANT OBJECTS 2026

SEASON 1

EDITED BY
ANDER MONSON

SIGNIFICANT OBJECTS 2026

SEASON 1

TUCSONESSAYCLUB.ORG/SIGNIFICANT-OBJECTS-2026/

NEW MICHIGAN PRESS
DEPT OF ENGLISH, P. O. BOX 210067
UNIVERSITY OF ARIZONA
TUCSON, AZ 85721-0067

<http://newmichiganpress.com>

Orders and queries to <nmp@thediagram.com>.

ISBN 978-1-971740-05-8. FIRST PRINTING.

Design and most photographs by Ander Monson.

<https://tucsonessayclub.org/significant-objects-2026/>

CONTENTS

About Significant Objects 2026

Significant Objects 2026 Season One began as a collaborative project for my Spring 2026 Advanced Fiction Workshop at the University of Arizona. I'd done this project, a reboot of the 2009 Significant Objects project organized by Joshua Glenn and Rob Walker (see more about the OG project at significantobjects.com), already during the pandemic in 2020, but at a small scale. As I thought about this project in Sprign 2026, I thought it might be fun to ask some of the writers we were reading in this class to contribute if it sounded fun to them. Many of them immediately said yes. A few said hell yes. Some were too busy or had too many other projects of their own. But most of them said yeah, I love objects; this sounds fun; let's do it.

Let me step back a moment to explain what Significant Objects 2026 *is*, for those of you who are encountering it for the first time in this book. Significant Objects 2026 comes out of a literary and publishing experiment in narrative and value. We ask: *what value does narrative add to an object? And how can we measure that?* 45 writers (16 of my students + myself and a bunch of other writer friends and acquaintances) each purchased or otherwise acquired objects secondhand for less than $5, wrote about them, and published the stories as auction listings on ebay. The winner of the auction received the object and a limited edition print of the story. My students decided that the proceeds from this project (and this book) would go to the Hermitage Cat Shelter, a local cat shelter in Tucson where my family has adopted four cats (and a few of these writers also have).

These 45 stories, poems, and essays explore the hidden lives of objects and their provenances. They're also a collaborative experiment in DIY publishing, which I've been increasingly inclined towards in recent years. Instead of submitting these stories to magazines and waiting for a year for the editors to find them in the slush pile, we published them ourselves directly to the people, roughly one a day during March, April, and May 2026. Auctions were only up seven days, so if you blinked, as many of us do, on account of there's a lot going on in the world and in our lives that all demands our attention, you might miss a story and its object. So I thought it would be a good idea to collect them, and the objects they describe, here in more lasting fashion in this volume you are holding.

We don't have enough data as of this printing to evaluate the success of the project, except to say that all the objects that have sold have sold for more than we paid for them. Narrative works. How well, we'll have to wait and see for the data to come in. But of course the real success of the project is bringing such an interesting crew of writers and makers together to do something collectively and to bring some joy into our lives. I hope you enjoy it!

As I mentioned, the Significant Objects 2026 project is ongoing, so if you're interested in collaborating be in touch! (You can find me at ander@arizona.edu.)

We have a number of other writers in the queue, but I wanted to print this book to celebrate the end of my students' and my semester together. So this includes the first 45 objects we put up for auction, listed alphabetically by writer's last name, and the accompanying stories, essays, or poems.

Most writers I know, and most of the people I care about love at least some objects. Objects have histories and residues of attention, as Jessica Oreck, writer and filmmaker and proprietor of the fantastic Office of Collection and Design (OCD), puts it. (You should check out her fantastic work and her traveling museum if you get the chance.) Objects might themselves have dreams or we might dream about them. How many objects do you have that simply remind you of an experience or of a person or of time that is otherwise lost to you? How powerful do objects become as they focus memory or emotion, as they remind us of who and what we used to be? Perhaps, objects tell us, we are still who we used to be. Perhaps we contain those selves, and the selves that imagine other possibilities and stories that have brought objects to us or animated them.

We live in the age of the new, everything disposable and shiny. Your iPhone is eligible for an upgrade, and, lo, in fact requires it. We face enshittification and planned obsolescence everywhere, and the pace of this appears to be increasing year after year. Folks my age know it. Gen Z knows it. Can a story rescue an object from obsolescence? Can an essay demonstrate objects' previous lives? Can narrative juice our interest in and love for objects? How can objects inspire stories, or vice versa? And what significance do stories carry?

Some writers chose to write from the POV of the object, or to discuss its provenance. Some made possibly outlandish claims about their objects that are likely unsubstantiatable. They could be true, I think. Fiction is just nonfiction that hasn't happened yet, my friend Nicole Walker tells me. I think a lot about a webshop I follow, Fugitive Kat Creations, which specializes in Haunted Dolls. I should put quotation marks around "Haunted," because it's not easy to substantiate how haunted most dolls are. I like dolls, and I discovered this shop several years ago as I was following a research rabbit hole down, and I talked with its proprietor. Each doll in her shop has an often quite long narrative attached, and they are provided with an entirely straight face. She has no time for people who just find dolls creepy in a horror movie way, and she has no time for anyone who doesn't believe, at least a little. It's hard to believe at least a little, I think, most days, but I'm trying.

—Ander Monson, April 2026

WORLD CHAMPIONSHIP
JULY
1-2-3-4

World Championship Timber Carnival 1983 Pin by Alisa Alering

You know how when you were a kid everybody got a label? My sister Karen was the Pretty One. And the Popular One. The Smart One. The Capable One. I'm Kimmy, the Quiet One. I liked to read books and pet the cat and climb up a tree and stay there all day. I liked watching people and places from the outside, thinking about how putting one thing next to another thing was terrible or beautiful or just somehow told the truth. I once saw a photo in Life magazine of a lady's hand and eye up close as she looked into a microscope and I couldn't stop thinking about it for days. I couldn't tell you why.

In 1983, I was fifteen and my whole family went to the Timber Carnival in Albany on the Fourth of July. Karen was seventeen and going to compete in the women's logrolling. The Grand Prize was $150. Karen said she was going to use it for her wedding, but I don't know who she thought she was going to marry, she didn't even have a boyfriend, which I don't blame her because all the boys around here didn't do anything but talk about Knight Rider and make AIDS jokes. Also did you know you can buy a Pentax K1000 camera for $150? It's true, I saw it in the JC Penney catalog.

Mom used to be a champion logroller. She met my dad at the 1960 Carnival, the first year they let women compete. Maybe mom was hoping Karen would meet someone too. She gave Karen her hand-me-down baseball cleats and had Dad and Uncle Ethan drag a big alder log into the irrigation pond and spent most of May and June teaching her how to do it. At first I just sat on the bank and watched. It was kind of fun seeing Karen not be great at something on the first try. It was definitely fun seeing Karen fall in the pond and come up covered in green goop, looking like a sick muskrat.

I wished I had a camera so I could take a picture of her dripping algae and pin it over the mirror of the dresser we shared, the slumped line of her wet shoulders showing what I knew about her but nobody else seemed to see. Karen wanted to quit, that was plain, but it wasn't in Karen's nature to let someone down so she kept getting up on that log getting madder and madder and falling down again and again. Finally Mom thought she'd had enough for one day and they went in to put the supper on for the men. Nobody ever paid attention to me so I waded out onto the log and gave it a try. I fell in, just like Karen. It was harder than it looked. But there was a rhythm to it. A way to kind of connect with the log, to its gravity or its mood and ride along with it. I can't really explain it. I'm not so good with words. More with pictures. But anyhow I could listen to the log it seemed.

The next day, I asked Mom if she would teach me too. I thought she was going to say no but then she shrugged and said she didn't see it would do any harm and maybe it would be something to have two champion log rollers in the family and that I could take over the title after Karen married and moved on. So I practiced with mom and sometimes I practiced with Karen but even though I sometimes ended up in the drink, Karen ended up there more. But it was like no one could see it.

Mom was so focused on Karen and Karen was so focused on being everything everyone wanted her to be that every time I was the one left standing alone on top the log with Karen flailing in the water below, they acted like it was a fluke, an accident, just one of those things. I guess I believed them. That's what happens when you're the youngest and everyone tells you how things are: we put ketchup on eggs, we say grace before dinner, animals are for outside, a girl can be as smart as a boy but she shouldn't show it. Dad is strong and brave and mom is dependable and your sister Karen is amazing. You are sweet, but you're not very good at things. Especially not useful things like school or sewing or fixing tractors or chopping firewood. But you're young still, maybe you'll grow into it eventually.

On the first of July mom loaded up the car with our tent and sleeping bags, boxes of cereal and crackers and the kind of cheese that sprays out of a can and we headed for Albany. I was thinking about the Ferris wheel and the fireworks and the Timber Queens in their sashes and when we bought our buttons, I pinned mine right on the front of my rainbow T-shirt. Mom went to the registration stand to enter Karen for the log rolling competition. At the last minute I asked mom to register me too and I was ready with a list of reasons why she should spend another two dollars, but she must have been in a party mood because she said what the heck, it would be good practice for me but to not pay any attention to the hoots of all the men when I fell in the water and came up dripping with my t-shirt all wet. I asked would they be boo-ing me and she gave me a funny look and said, not exactly, just never mind.

I wandered around the carnival while Karen made friends with kids from all over the state and even other countries, like this boy Iñaki, which is a name I never heard before because he is from Spain. It's a good name, I liked the way it tasted on my tongue, eeen-yah-kee, he was there because his dad was the #1 block chopper in the whole world. Our dad was competing in the springboard so that was okay because they weren't rivals. I saw Karen and Iñaki kissing behind the funnel cake stand. I guess she liked the way he tasted on her tongue too.

We watched the parade and the axe throwing and power sawing. When it came to the springboard, Dad did okay but his board got stuck and he didn't win and he had a few beers and sulked for a while until mom made a big deal over him he came back around and was there to cheer Karen on when it was time for the women's logrolling.

There was a pretty big crowd watching us and even a reporter there from CBS. Some of the girls weren't serious, you can tell they had barely practiced but some of them were tough, like this scary redhead from Yakima who chewed gum the whole match, like she wished she was chomping on my leg. The log roll is a two out of three so even if you lose the first go, you still have a chance. I got dunked a few times, but I won all my heats and so did Karen and then it was the finals and we were the only ones left.

The guy from CBS was exclaiming into his microphone: "This is for the ladies' championship." Karen and I climbed out on the log and we started rolling and I dropped Karen into the water in the first round. I couldn't believe it. Maybe I could win this thing, maybe I could have that prize money and get a camera of my own that I could hold up to the world and show what I saw when I was being quiet.

Karen crawled out of the water looking like a sick muskrat again and got back up on the log wringing water out of her ponytail and she waved to mom like it was okay, everything was fine, great, but she was talking to me in sister language with her eyes and what she was saying was "You are going to be sorry."

She put her head down then and we started rolling and she was mad and she was fast and I guess I was shook because this time I was the one splashing in the lake but it is hot in Oregon on the Fourth of July and I had been working hard so mostly it felt good when the water swallowed me. When I got back up on the log Karen was looking a lot happier, her eyes were saying, "Remember who's in charge here."

The CBS reporter said, "We'll go now for the third fall which will decide the logrolling champ for 1983. This will decide it." The referee asked if we were ready and I nodded yes and he counted down and we started rolling, my legs moving, and I was just in it not looking at my feet in their shoes and what they were doing and not really thinking about Karen and that log kept switching directions under me and I tipped forward but I got a grip and got back on top and Karen she kept up with me, she was good, really, I mean, she had knocked six other girls into the lake before me and she really didn't want to be beat by her sister on national TV but my focus then it just kind of zoomed and I was pedaling pedaling and the crowd was buzzing in my head. I don't know if they were shouting for me or against me or if they just liked seeing two girls in wet clothes running on top of a log.

And then Karen was gone, slipped off the log and into the water with barely a splash and I was balancing on the top and the man from CBS was yelling about a winner and mom had one hand over her mouth and that boy from Spain was looking disappointed. Through all this I kept standing there on the log and I felt good if a little surprised and then I realized that Karen hadn't come back up.

Was she mad at me? Did she swim away to the other shore so she wouldn't have to come up the loser in front of the whole wide world on CBS Sports? But then I saw mom was looking worried and so was Iñaki. Dad yelled something and I saw she was nowhere and I wondered what could have happened, the lake was not that deep but Karen was my sister so I jumped into the water and sucked in a big breath and ducked under the surface and the water was still cold but this time it didn't feel like a relief. It just felt icy and numb and I looked around, trying to see Karen through the murk.

Something in the water made a kind of tunnel and at the bottom of it far away like looking down the wrong end of binoculars there was Karen at the bottom and her lips were moving but I couldn't understand the sister language. I was hanging there in time and she was hanging there too and the whole crowd of people, mom and dad and Iñaki and the timber princesses and the CBS reporter and the cameraman who tried to pinch my bottom and the girl from the cotton candy stand, they were all somewhere far above and I was looking at Karen at the bottom of that tube in the water and she was tiny and manageable and nothing she could say could stop me and I knew then she wasn't going to bother me anymore. I was going to get that camera with the prize money and I was going to show the world what I could see. The fact that Karen once told the whole school that I drool in my sleep didn't matter at all. It didn't even matter that she broke Grandma's china rabbit and let me get punished for it or that when she had a bad day she punched me hard in the arm when no one was looking. None of it mattered when I looked down that long watery hole that she was stuck in and so I stretched my hand through the liquid aperture until I made contact with her pretty ankle in a baseball cleat and pulled her out, back to the surface.

An Insignificant Object (Rabbit Figurine) by Lofton Allen

It wasn't his fault. I know it couldn't have been. It's just a strange coincidence, that's all. Sometimes I can't help it, though. There are moments where I think that he had to have had some hand in it—what happened to my uncle. He's this strange ceramic rabbit that's poised and balanced just right so that he can sit on the edge of a shelf. I think he's strange at least. Strange in the way that it's strange how one can claim to not believe in monsters or ghosts or the boogie man or whatever you want to call it, but is still afraid in an otherwise empty house after the sun goes down. It's his purpose to observe from somewhere high up, to watch, even if it may not look like that's what he's doing.

It appears as though his eyes are closed, but I don't believe it. He has this smile too. It's this terrible grin that winds across his face from one side to the other. I can't look at him for long. It just feels like he's peering at me from behind those heavy lids, and I can't see his pupils. It's similar to when you talk to someone and they're wearing sunglasses but you aren't, and so there's this imbalance. If the eyes are the windows to anything—the soul they often say, but who knows really—then the one wearing the sunglasses can see deep into yours while your view of theirs is strictly prohibited by the dark, reflective, glass abyss. With the rabbit though, he doesn't need glasses. He just peers at you through those unseen eyes. Even if I could see his pupils; if I were privy to his windows, I don't know that there'd be anything there.

I know this is all, really, quite silly to say—to admit maybe—I just can't shake the feeling. I know that he's just a shelf decoration. I understand that. But I can't explain the change.

As I said, it was my uncle. Or, I guess he wasn't really my uncle, not by blood at least, but for simplicity's sake that's what you can think of him as. Walt was his name. He'd always been kind of enigmatic, I suppose. Maybe eccentric, but whatever he was, he had a knack for attracting the bizarre. He had all kinds of collections—playboys, sunglasses, bottles that he'd fill with shards of glass he'd find on the beach that'd been smoothed over after being brutalized by the waves, diner mugs, lots of stuff from his travels to all kinds of places. And he almost always had an interesting "lady friend" hanging around. He never used the word girlfriend, and if you did, he'd correct you. He'd been alone for a while before bringing home the rabbit.

One day he just came home with the thing. It was well dressed in a blue jacket, white pants, a little handkerchief, and had this green book resting on his chest. A book of which no one knows the origin or contents of, except him. Upon encountering the little thing—he is little, probably only four inches tall—you feel that he's privy to something of which you can never be. That's not just because of the book though. I already told you about the look. Anyway, my uncle called him . Walt brought the little thing home about two months ago I guess it was. I went over to his place for dinner about a day or so after he got it and he made this big deal about showing me. It was strange though. It almost felt more like he was showing me to the rabbit, as opposed to showing the rabbit to me. He said he was going to start this new collection and he just went on and on about how he couldn't believe the "spirit" of it. I thought the thing was creepy from go, and I told him that—we could always be honest with one another, Walt and I—but he insisted that I respect and use his name. I don't know where Walt got the name. So strange. I only saw him a few more times after that.

The next time I saw him he was noticeably thinner and had bags under his eyes. I assumed he'd just not been sleeping all that well. He'd had a way of throwing himself into different projects and hyper focusing on things to the point where he'd forget to eat and/or not want to sleep or whatever. But then we started talking. He'd always been obsessive, but this was something else. He was paranoid. He said he couldn't get over the feeling that he was being watched. He said that his friends were plotting against him. Even I'd had to convince him pretty hard to let me come over. He said he'd started confiding in about his deepest thoughts. It was the only way he felt safe, he said. Said that the trinket was speaking to him. He didn't say "trinket" of course. He spoke about it like it was human.

Seeing Walt again after that, he was worse. He wouldn't even talk to me; he'd only write things down and give them to me to read. He wouldn't let me talk either. Apparently "he" was listening, but Walt wouldn't tell me who, because "he'd know," and that would be "very very bad." I didn't know what he was talking about. I do now. I didn't stay for long because the house had started to smell, and he didn't have any food anyway even though we'd planned on having dinner.

The last time I saw him he was dead. I'd rather not say how I found him. There was a note. All it said was "It's true. I'm convinced. I believe." over and over until you couldn't really read his writing. Apparently he'd planned it all out too, because he'd even revised his will. All that the new version said was that he left to me and that he'd already freed himself of all other worldly things. His last days were spent in an empty house, though to say he was alone may not be quite right.

I took the rabbit home, but I can't keep him. I know it was Walt's last wish, but I can't do it. It's almost like I feel what he felt, and after what I saw—. I just can't. Something doesn't feel right about throwing him out though, and I'm not totally convinced he'd stay gone if I were to just discard him anyway. I also don't think I can just give him away. That wouldn't be fair. If you desire him enough to buy, be my guest. To list him as "free" and pass him along to someone I've never met who would presumably take the "freeness" to mean that he is just some insignificant object would be an act of deep and terrible deceit. Even though I know that's exactly what he is. He has to be. I know he couldn't have had anything to do with what happened. Not really.

Summit House

Pike's Peak Perfect Crime (Summit House Shot Glass) by Brisa Bejarano

I found this in my partner's apartment. It was a few years ago, a few years after undergrad. He was washing dishes as I was drying, and putting them in their respective place in the cupboard. I reached for the shot glass he had just placed on the rack, and examined it. It occurred to me that I hadn't seen it before, or if I had, I hadn't given it much thought. I read the words "Summit House" on one side, and noticed the monorail display. I turned the thing over, and rubbed the red letters with my thumb.

"Pike's Peak" I read aloud. "When did you go to Colorado?" I turned to him.

"Huh?" His head pivoted to me. "Oh," He let out a laugh, and I found a glimmer of youth in his eyes. He took a moment to smile before he spoke.

"In college, I started playing this game with myself. Every house party I went to, I gave myself a mission to steal at least one thing. It was usually a shot glass or lighter," His smile was warm as he returned to the soapy sink in front of him.

It was kind of the perfect crime. These items are not big enough, significant enough, to notice its disappearance or to mark it as theft. I squinted at him, wondering if he had ever stolen anything from me. We met in college, at one of my parties actually, and on my favorite holiday. Red and pink streamers hung from the ceiling, and heart-shaped confetti was strewn across the floor. I swear, I could still find pieces of it in that house today, if I looked hard enough. Candy hearts with silly sayings like "All yours" or "Choke me" and love letters were plastered all over the walls that night. I saw him for the first time under the purple lights.

"No, I never stole from you," he assured, glancing back at me. Dishes clanked as he moved them around. My squint subsided, but I wasn't satisfied with just that.

"Why this shot glass specifically?" I asked. "And who did you steal it from?"

"Oh, Missy, I don't know. It was a long time ago. It's all blurry from the alcohol and other stuff. I really can't say."

I kept a blank stare on him, long enough for him to do a double-take.

"It was something small enough to fit in my pocket," He chuckled.

I looked back down to the thing in my hand. It's unlike any shot glass made in the last ten or maybe twenty years. The design seemed more intentional than that. It's a bit heavier on the bottom, with more attention to detail. The words "I made it!" plastered across it. I wondered about the previous owner and the view they must have seen at Summit House.

"I'm just surprised I didn't know about this before."

"Don't be, Missy," He kissed me softly on the cheek. His lips were warm and comforting like a blanket. I showed him my dimples before returning to my task.

My imagination ran rampant. I wondered and fabricated memories to string myself along. The path started from the moment my partner took the shot glass, likely before our paths even crossed, yet I saw it so clearly. He's at a party, and his eyes are all glossy from the joint he just shared on the apartment's cold and quiet balcony. He's all smiley, too. He stumbles in the kitchen with his roommate, Theo, and finds the display of used shot glasses on the table.

"You should take one," Theo nudges.

They glance over to the host, a girl he has lab with on Monday and Wednesday evenings. She's singing that Chainsmokers song at the top of her lungs, and he slips the shotglass into his jacket's pocket. He gives one last look to Theo, their grins are sneaky and full of understanding.

Upon seeing this first shot glass, I began to question how my partner acquired the rest of his belongings. He danced around the topic like jumping through clouds, I had to admire this about him. I still do, even after finding my lighter in his car.

Eat Bugs (Papier-Mache Baby in Golden Robes) by Sarah Blackman

There was a child walking down the middle of the road. Toddling, Colleen amended, taking in the child's spraddle-legged stagger, the unsteady girth of its head. She tutted to herself and snapped the blue rubber band she wore loose around her wrist. Even now, in extremity—the child clearly too young to be left to its own devices; the road not busy, but not abandoned; the day too far along to be considered wholly innocent to its outcome—she could not help but be what Dr. Burgess had long ago determined was, "hyper-fixated on a presumption of control expressed through lingual neurosis among other complications." Colleen had snuck a peek at Dr. Burgess' notes. She had been twenty-two, so fresh and dewy. Daddy was footing the bill.

But that had shut her up, hadn't it? Presumption more than any other word. Daddy more than Dr. Burgess who would turn in this report to her father seated at his historically accurate replica of John Jacob Astor's writing desk from behind which JJA had penned the notes that sent opium to China and ordered a generation of beavers to grace the heads of Europe's elite. Also from behind which Daddy, not John Jacob nor Dr. Burgess, would determine whatever he determined, the outcome of which was to keep Colleen at home. Homebound. Home biddy. No matter. Daddy had other daughters and the house was spacious and familiar. In the street, the child struggled to balance head, belly, bottom. It lifted one stiff leg and pivoted. It flung out its arms.

Presumption, hypothesis, axiom. If one followed the breadcrumbs long enough, most words became certainties. But that wasn't how Dr. Burgess saw her. Not scientific *(scholarly, erudite)* but emotional *(histrionic, incandescent)* which was the worst thing, the very worst thing, a woman *(a doll, a valentine)* could be. Nor was it how Daddy took it, which was badly, but with a frisson of relief. It helped that Colleen was the youngest child, the other two safely married. She was also the one who most resembled Daddy in physicality. She had Daddy's large, grey eyes which yellowed in his later years as if what was most vital in them had been preserved under a layer of curdling aspic. She had his scoliatic posture *(lordotic, hunchback),* his spindly shanks and very handsome ankles. Was it like keeping himself at home? A younger, poorer, weaker, more secret self, kept tucked at home next to his heart and snot-stiff pocket handkerchief? Well, what had Daddy known? Not everything. Not that much.

Swift, swift, swift, swift, Colleen used to say to herself when she was a child, sauntering along the upstairs' landing, admiring the flash of white above her shoe where her stocking clung. "What's that? What's that you are mumbling out there?" Daddy shouted from the parlor, his bedroom, the library, his study where he hunched behind John Jacob's desk accounting for the 86,000 spindles that filled Petty Mills with humming. He could not know her velocity, that was for sure. Her *(celerity, rapidity, tempo, reel).* That her mother was only briefly in the picture should come as no surprise. More than the other two girls, who chittered and flitted, she had Daddy's fondness for silence *(comity, concord);* yet, of the three girls it was her little noises that bothered Daddy the most. "A mewly child," he had described her not so very long before he finally died, but Colleen did not let the vagueness of that label bother her. She was the last, after all. Last one born; only one left. Even the mill was a rubble now, and the house, and the garden.

Colleen broke the desiccated head of a summer-struck hydrangea off in her fist *(grip, glove, grasp).* The garden was dry, gasping. It rustled against itself and also rustled with the sunbaked chomp of the enormous grasshoppers that appeared this time of year, humping on the front porch steps, lumbering around in the lavender. Daddy had called them lubbers, but she herself had always favored the name the generals (standard-bearers, czars) and could not stand to see them, but also could not stand to crush them, as Daddy sometimes did, beneath her shoe. She had been alive for far too long, and yet, here she was, still living. She snapped the rubber band against her wrist. A general buzzed its short, stubby wings. In the street, the child crowed.

“What’s that? What’s that?” Colleen said to the child, but it did not repeat itself. They were closer together, now. Colleen had come partly down the gentle slope in the front garden and was gripping the wrought-iron garden fence, each hand just below a wicked garden spike. The child had spun in place, stumbled a few steps further, plumped on its rump next to the faded dotted line that signified the middle of the road, neither here nor there. Colleen pushed through the day lilies. Ever social, they flung their unpleasant odor up in her face and smeared her gardening smock with their pollen (microspore, gamete, sperm). “Phew, you bitches. Take it away, you sluts,” Colleen commented. Daddy liked the tender flowers better—shy ones, downcast mumblers. *Should I pluck the lilly-of-the-valley?* she had often commented in Daddy’s hearing, *should I strip the bellwort, raze the groundsel, reap the phlox?* The garden was her domain.

“Yes, yes, Colleen,” Daddy had soothed (consoled, allayed, reformed), “Yes, yes, it is a pretty day.”

On closer inspection, the child was only a little more than a baby. Its hair was thick and dark, but lifted at its neck and behind its ears in the weightless curls of infancy. Its lips were as puckered as an opening bud; its eyes fringed by long, shy lashes that reminded her, for some reason, of a giraffe’s knees carefully emphasized in a picture book. “Baboo,” the baby said, or some such utterance. There were sores on its chin and around its mouth which had crusted over with a thick, honey-colored crust. Someone had cut a hole in the center of a yellow towel and slipped it over the baby’s head so the towel flapped over the baby’s body in the loose drapery of vestment *(caparison, toggery, cloth of gold)* beneath which the baby appeared to be entirely in the nude.

Colleen inched her way toward the garden gate, post-by-post. A cluster of generals, all facing in different directions as they chewed, lurched reluctantly from beneath her questing feet. They radiated like a tattered fan, spreading with raddled symmetry through the undergrowth. Daddy had died twenty years ago, maybe twenty-five. He lived long enough to see his empire go to ruin, as John Jacob Astor had not, but not quite long enough to go down with the ship, as John Jacob Astor’s great-grandson had, and as Colleen herself would happily *(jocularly, rapturously, giggling, elated)* should the great, grey, unwieldy, peeling, scabrous legacy of the Petty family's textile conglomerate ever roll its barnacled belly toward the sky and slip beneath the waves. As it was, the mills closed, then burned, then lay dormant for ten, fifteen, twenty-five years before the property was sold and reimagined as eleven acres of loft-style living, Astroturfed dog parks, artisanal taco stands every Thursday night. The house endured, crumbling at its corner—more rain-spotted, more racoon-looted, emptying but not empty. The garden grew in wild riot.

And Colleen *(Cailín, Cailleach, countrywoman, wench)* had she not also rioted? Thrown the plate upon the floor *(really, Colleen, control yourself)*, ripped them hem from the skirt *(this kind of behavior, my dear, only proves my point)*, pressed the tines of the serving fork into the soft, white skin of her own raw thigh *(what would your mother think, if she could see you now?)*. In her youth, Colleen was no shy understory plant, no blushing mumbler. She had lifted her skirts, dropped her knickers, climbed the pear tree, howled at the chimney pots. No matter. When the generals came in the summer they chomped every plant down to its roots regardless of floral temperament. The house still stood. Even with Daddy gone, Colleen remained at home while the neighborhood evolved from grand manors to subdivided ranches; from post-war families to malingering, slat-toothed great-grands; from commodious pots for plump chickens to government cheese. All to say, a child lost in the middle of the street was not the strangest thing to be seen. Not the most unsavory *(revolting, insipid, foul)*. Not the least divine.

Colleen crept to the gate and inched it open. The creak was pleasing, a grating sound that flaked with rust. Younger had she clung to this self-same gate, thrusting her belly against the posts like a frog, for the bedevilment *(vexation, torment)* of the mailman? Of course, she had. By what other means could Daddy and all his many decisions be reified? She was the youngest daughter—lovely Mary dead in childbirth; furious Laura straight-jacketed to her own house and husband, sons and garden in another neighborhood in another town. She was the only one left to gleep at Daddy's feet and make him wonder. Out loud. (O God why has thou….*inflicted*….me?)

Now, too, Colleen would like to cling; not so much has changed. Not the gate itself, not the generations of day lilies stinking upon the land. But her body has changed, yes. More crooked *(sinuous, jagged, crazy),* more craggy *(serrated, roughened, irregular),* more prone to break *(explode, wreck, bomb).* The threadbare carpet of the future unravels down the future's long hall. "One more bad fall," the doctor (not Burgess) had said, "and you'll no longer be able to live alone." I have never lived alone, Colleen replied, though not in so many words. I have never been anything but *en masse.*

However, Colleen admitted, there was also the grate of the gate, the susurration of her slipper, the unwieldly leap of the generals, the baby in the street. Those things which were not her must also have their due. She was fair-minded when she had to be. She was clement, peaceable, serene. In this condition, the baby saw her coming. It raised its arms and flexed its hands. "Gimme gimme," Colleen said, inching forward. From across the street, a neighbor shouted, "Hey! Whose kid is that?" Together they made a triangle, a tightening shape that converged on a point. Colleen, enrobed babe, the neighbor (a grizzled semi-stranger whose brick rambler was varyingly draped in blue tarps and nets of ivy) considered each other over the interluding asphalt. A general tromped out of the garden verge and stood bold upon the street, balancing on the very tips of its fine, articulate, bristling, yellow, segmented, hair-thin toes. Colleen snapped and snapped her rubber band. The baby began to cry.

Daddy's obsession with John Jacob Astor had come upon him in the middle of his life. He was floundering; he needed direction and settled on back. "Early on, Astor recognized the frailty of a goods-based economy," Daddy vented, hands clasped behind him, monologuing before the fire. Lovely Mary, twelve years older, knelt beside Colleen to help her untangle the ribbon from her gift. Was this Christmas morning, then; a birthday? Was the box a velvet one and inside was there an iron key? "The insufferable tendency of the beaver to decline! The willful frippery of fashion! The dwindling crescendo of bliss!" Daddy proclaimed *(heralded, hierophized)*. Did he rock back and forth on his splendid toes? There, before his daughters, did he profess? "Don't worry, Colly," Mary said. "No one is angry with you." Lovely Mary—had she lived she would be dead. Perhaps the baby as well, by now. So many years whirred by like the spokes on the wheels of the tiny toy train Daddy set to spin around the Christmas tree. Laura gone (who cared, she pinched) and Mary; Daddy, too, but not Colleen who spun and spun and spun in place. "Astor pivoted," Daddy concluded. "He diversified to real estate, where the real money lay. He encouraged the land to shake hands with itself."

"Alright, then" said Laura, "let's get on with it. Won't somebody cut the cake?"

"What's that?" the neighbor asked. He stuck out one beefy (lumpish, clumsy) hand and, when she did not take it, slid her hand into his own like a child's chilblained paw into a mitten. "Name's Greavy. Don't think we've met."

"Uh uh wah," the baby cried, not yet despairing. The general stared stiffly forward from behind its mystifying eye. It had tramped all the way to the edge of baby's towel and placed one foreleg on the towel's fringe. Its trajectory *(pretension, prerogative)* from there was unclear, almost assuredly to itself as well as onlookers, but its progress seemed certain. Up and down, the sweep of street remained stubbornly empty. Colleen's own home *(domicile, villa, manse)* squatted amongst the gardens, the ersatz orchard, the outbuildings overcome by creeper and tall, feathery dog fennel, taking up the entire block. Across the way, this Greavy's house was centered on Colleen's own front door, their front doors facing as if one house were making a face in the other house's mirror. Were Colleen to go into this Greavy's back yard would she see the horseshoe trace of the carriage loop that had once circled *(girdled, ringed)* both properties? Would she find the dumbstruck trunk of the illustrious oak that had once marked its center? "Horses can't back up, Colleen," Daddy said to explain the track's ambling largesse. "To travel by horse and carriage is to commit to looking indefinitely ahead."

"Did you see where it came from?" the neighbor asked. He looked down at the baby, now 'gimme

gimme'-ing its hands at him, face beginning to crumple in serious sorrow. Colleen considered. She took her time. Bearded, hair thin on top, paunchy, sweaty, his forearms a thicket of wiry reddish fur, this Greavy stood like a man about to flip over a brick to see what wriggled. A man about to nudge a baby with his toe. He wore khaki cargo shorts, the pockets stuffed with varying shapes, and a blue bandana tied around his wrist. A carpenter's pencil was tucked behind his ear. The houses on either side of Greavy's own were similarly brick, similarly slumping, but seemed perhaps abandoned—windows broken, a screen door hanging from its hinge—while Greavy's tarps were snug, his nets of ivy cut at the base to wither, his porch sanded with sawdust and yellow boards showing on the eves. A homesteader, then, Colleen dismissed him; a settler recolonizing the ruins of the plains.

Much more interesting: the baby with its golden cloak and blameless cheek. The attendant general was whirring now on baby's ankle where the pricking of its thumbs caused babe to wail in earnest, a lamentation cast across the neighborhood like a sudden flash of light. How many years had it been since Colleen had teetered on this side of the gate? The train set flashed its fancy wheels, puffed its intemperate chest. Colleen stooped, or planned to stoop. She gestured with her knees toward the baby who turned again to her the lighthouse of its gaze, each window-eye suffused with water. Of all the art Daddy kept in replica, the Pieta in the morning garden was Colleen's most beloved. She crept (she *crouched*, she *wormed*, she *wriggled*, she *snuck)* there even still to touch the intelligent veins that crossed the tops of Christ's feet, to nestle in the monumental drapery that clothed his mother's knee. Lovely Mary looked down so beaming at her growing belly. "We'll name him Donald if it's a boy. If it's a girl, then maybe Callie. Would you like that, pet?" A pet, a dear, a precious, a sweet. Born to suffer, to writhe, to keen.

"What's that?" Daddy shouted down from the veranda. "What are you doing down there on your knees? You'll get your pinny dirty, girl. You're going to make a mess." Where was anybody's mother in these stories? Colleen wondered. Mary waited so patiently to hold her son across her knee. Colleen extended one knobbed knuckle downward. She would *(could, may, might, possibly, is conceivable, is not forbidden, her will decrees)* stroke a baby's cheek.

"Woah there," that Greavy said and gripped her at the elbow. "You wanna sit down somewhere? You need something to drink?"

John Jacob Astor's great-grandson, himself a JJA, this one the fourth, was an historically insignificant byline *(curio, trivia),* an abbreviated ellipsis. When Daddy began to get woeful about legacy, his thoughts turned to fancies of death at sea. "A gentleman to the end, he hoisted his pregnant wife into the Titanic's lifeboat and stood aside," Daddy mourned, sipping the steam off his toddy. "When they recovered his body—the richest man in the world!—it was marked by the effects of the water, and only his possessions were left to identify the remains. A golden pocket watch, a monogrammed handkerchief, a brown flannel shirt with JJA stitched on the back collar. His fine moustache was hung with icicles beneath the ruin of his face."

Daddy had done his research, but grew more fanciful the fewer people there were to hear the telling. Some daughters dead, staff dismissed, Colleen herself not quite the human *(hominid, anthropoid, earthborn)* he had envisioned to carry on the Petty name. Daddy waxed peculiar and outside the seasons changed as they always had, the street carved through their estate filled and emptied, houses eyed each other across their fences, neighbors ravaged the vestal night. "Our only safety lies in numbers, Colly," Lovely Mary had once said. But did she mean the safety of gentry, the safety of daughters, the safety of children which it is unendurable to harm unless by sacrifice the greater good washes clean its crimson hands? Colleen did not mistake the way the baby *had not* cried until there was a witness *(bystander, spy)* to its distress. More, the way the baby *had not* been distressed until there was a receptacle which would fill with reciprocal anguish. "Just wait," she whispered, not unkindly. "You have no *(idea, hypothesis, fancy).* You have no *(speculation, prejudice, conceit)*."

"You're in it, huh?" said Greavy. He hauled her upright and tucked her arm beneath the pinion of his own, pointing to the rubber band which Colleen had faithfully *(fatefully)* continued to snap. "I was there once, too," he continued. He was wearing thick-framed rectangular glasses behind which his thick-lashed rectangular eyes slatted in sympathy. "What's your poison? Mine was cigarettes, then biting my nails when I had that kicked. I'd just get in there and chaw them down. Blood on my teeth. Chew my hand right off, I thought. I beat it, though. Look at me now."

Colleen looked. The same, this Greavy, as he had been. A red t-shirt stretched across his belly, the painful extrusion of a sty empurpling the underlid of one brown eye. She looked at his fingers where they manacled her arm—all of them still there, none of them gnawed more brief. A liar, then; a thief, Colleen concluded. I Do No Eat Ze Bugs, Greavy's t-shirt read. If Collen were given the task of naming all the animals Baby would be Eat Bugs, Greavy would be Grieve, she herself: Divine Hag, who was once Beloved, Bitter Woman, Drop of the Sea. Colleen knew herself to be terrible at choices *(designations, patronyms).* Daddy, and Dr. Burgess, had told her so. She suffered as she had always suffered: in the middle of all things. Nevertheless, Collen had done her own research. Aboard the Titanic were many who sacrificed, who stood in a circle and prayed as the waters rose. Many who drifted face-down bobbing into ice bergs. The massive plinth of ice that rose above them; the massive plinth of ship that sank below. But Daddy only marked the one lost scion, not even the babe born later who bore exactly his father's name. Daddy was only interested in the moment, not in the long long silence that came after. Colleen knew better—the present tense was an additive present, a scavenge of parts They three in the street, the triumvirate *in perpetua*—Smooth-Tongued Grief, the Bitter Woman, the Hungry Child—would break apart at the slightest shift of the tides. They were a happenstance assemblage; they could drift into any number of shapes.

Then, to Colleen's surprise and without losing track of her brittle arm, Greavy stooped and scooped the baby up as if it were no more than a raucous kitten and shuffled it one-handed against his chest. The baby hiccupped *(caesuraed, lagged),* tears tracking into the corners of its mouth and making its scintillate, honey-sores glisten. Its towel rucked up to reveal the flourishing podge of its thighs. *Eat bugs, eat bugs,* Colleen enchanted. Ascendant on baby's knee the general stood at parade rest, surveying its vast battleground, eyes forward, mandibles aclick. Colleen paused a moment to admire the burnished orange and luminous yellow of its uniform, the speckle of its epaulettes, the startling crimson of its inner wing. "Oops, hang on," Greavy interjected and released her just long enough to swat the general and send him flying. "Got to get those fuckers before they spit," he said. The sun above the road had not moved one bit and never did. It was she herself who was spinning.

"Baboo," said Eat Bugs, once again.

Collen stretched out her wavering (hesitant, skeptical) hand (appendage, ornament) and stroked (caressed, gentled) the baby's (moppet, nursling, cherub, splendor, joy and rescue, darkness and light) cheek.

At the top of the street, a woman appeared who, as she ran toward them, began to scream.

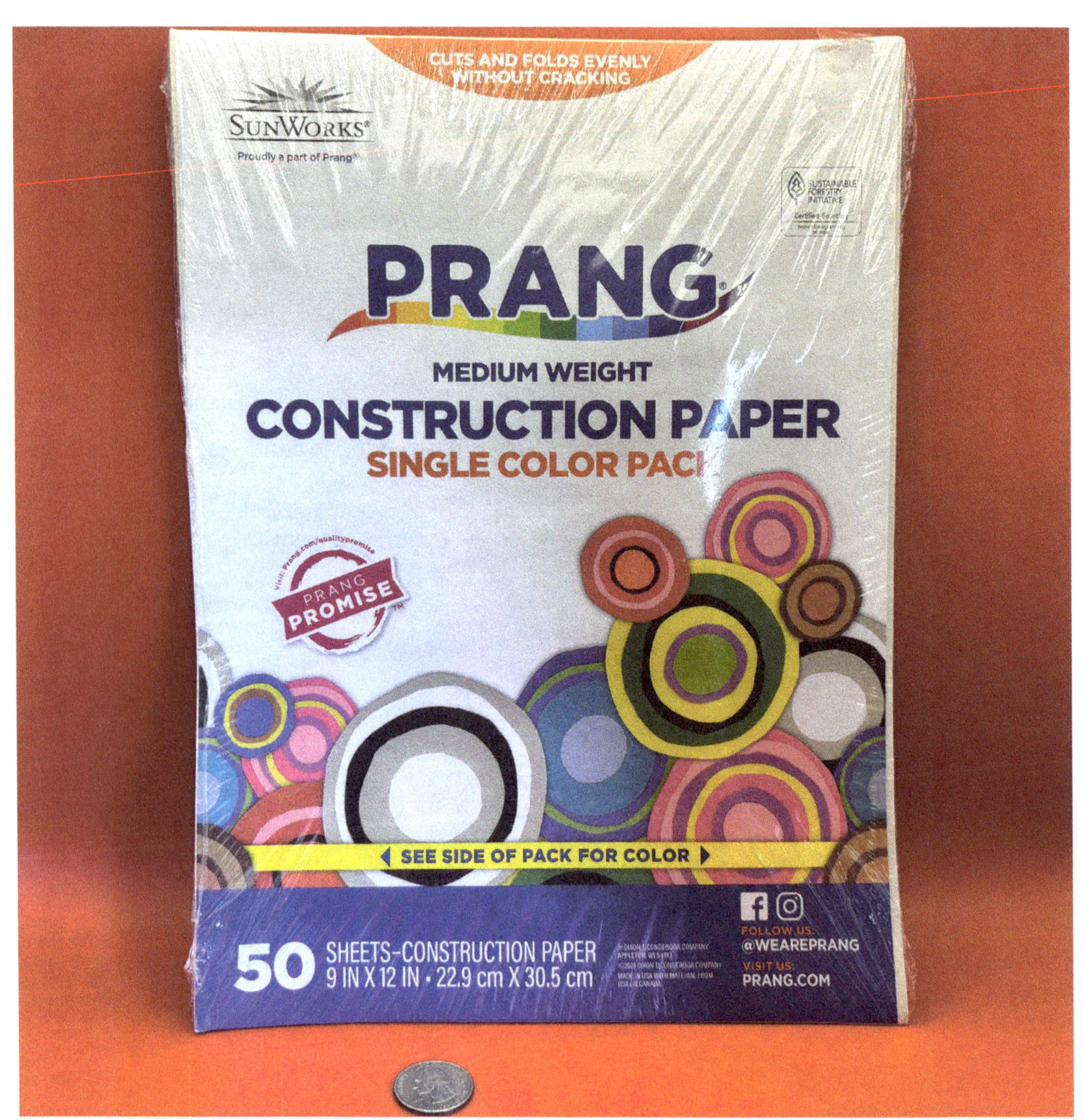
CUTS AND FOLDS EVENLY
WITHOUT CRACKING
SUNWORKS®
Proudly a part of Prang®
SUSTAINABLE FORESTRY INITIATIVE
PRANG®
MEDIUM WEIGHT
CONSTRUCTION PAPER
SINGLE COLOR PAC
Visit: Prang.com/qualitypromise
PRANG PROMISE™
SEE SIDE OF PACK FOR COLOR
50 SHEETS-CONSTRUCTION PAPER
9 IN X 12 IN · 22.9 cm X 30.5 cm
FOLLOW US:
@WEAREPRANG
VISIT US:
PRANG.COM

White Paper by Megan Campbell

Ainsley was quite young when she realized that people were not very observant. In fact, most people struck her as terribly *unobservant*. Odd things, even impossible things, would slip right past them, particularly if the things were strange or spectral or upsetting, and even more particularly if the things somehow benefitted them. From age nine until age eleven she assiduously filled the family saltshaker with salt from the big red box in the pantry; no one ever commented or even seemed to notice (though the red box was regularly replaced). Did they not wonder why the saltshaker was always full? Did it not feel like a miracle?

A miracle. She thought about miracles a lot. The salt wasn't a miracle, just a prank, but what if other things were happening, unnoticed and unremarked upon? Could real miracles be happening every day, under the noses of people who simply didn't perceive them? Young Ainsley vowed to be the one who noticed everything.

She waited and watched throughout her childhood and teenage years, but the only miracles she witnessed were the product of her own hand. She slyly changed the magnet holding the syllabus onto the file cabinet next to her favorite teacher's desk every week throughout freshman year, but he never commented. She rearranged the collection of family photos on the hall table at least once a month. Junior year, she arrived at swim practice early every morning and placed one of the thin bleached school towels in front of each swimmer's locker. Nothing.

In college she was assigned a work-study job at the campus copy center. After a month or two, she finally noticed something. One of the copiers never needed paper. She'd never filled it or seen anyone else fill it either. She wasn't there all the time, but at some point its emptiness should have coincided with her shift. She watched for two weeks before trying to pry it open and look inside. Max saw her.

"Oh, that one's full," he said.

"Did you just fill it" she asked, trying to repress her excitement.

"No, I can just tell from the sound," he replied. He thumped the paper tray with his fist. "See? Sounds full."

Ainsley started watching the machine closely. Along with never needing paper, it never broke down, or ran out of ink, or made weird noises. One day as she stood over it, waiting for 50 copies of a psych test to emerge, she leaned in close and whispered, "I see you."

The next night she and Max worked until closing. They had turned out the lights and shut down the machines so that desperate passing students would realize they were out of luck (still the beseeching faces pressed themselves upon the locked glass doors). Max had worked there longer and thus had the better task — doing inventory in the stockroom - while she wiped the counters and swept the floor. As she pushed the broom in front of the mystery machine it suddenly lit up and thrummed loudly.

Ainsley jumped. It was turned off, for sure—she'd done it herself. It continued thrumming, somehow faster and louder than normal, a mechanical purr or growl. She heard the familiar sound of a piece of paper being carried through its innards, even though there was nothing to copy. It spit the page out and went quiet. She picked it up. On it was a single sentence:

You sang while we burned.

"Ready?" Max called, closing the stockroom door. Startled, she dropped the broom.

"Sorry. Yeah, ready," she replied, slipping the paper under her sweater as she bent to retrieve the broom.

Ainsley traded shifts with her coworkers so she could close as many times as possible over the next week. Two nights later she was back, anxiously waiting for Sascha to check the stock room. The overhead fluorescents were off and the copy center glowed with a faint green light as she did a desultory pass with the broom. She'd double-checked the off switch on every copier and was working the broom into the farthest corner when she heard the thrum.

Another piece of paper in the tray, a copy of nothing.

You will eat and eat until you eat the whole world.

Ainsley shuddered. Sascha slammed the stock room door. "Those are supposed to be off," she said crankily.

Ainsley couldn't get a closing shift for three days. She was anxious, jumpy. She forgot to notice things. It occurred to her that anything could be happening, miracles exploding everywhere, and she would have missed them. This only increased her anxiety. *Can one miracle hide behind another? How much can the human brain even comprehend?*

In her calmer moments she considered the possibility of a prankster, maybe even someone like her. Sascha was a dullard, the least compelling person she knew, but Max was clever. He seemed to like her, too. Her mind churned.

The evening shift arrived. Four tedious hours of copying tests, worksheets. She used the special printer as much as possible, paying attention to every aspect of it. It worked perfectly. It gave no sign. Max got bogged down by an ancient, wizened professor demanding hand-outs in multiple colors, and she ducked into the stock room and rearranged several reams of paper. He was a stickler; she would gain precious private minutes with the copier.

Waiting for 9pm was agony. At 8:59 she was able to lock the door, practically in the face of some volleyball girls clutching a flyer. *Too bad.* Max looked at her oddly as he headed for the stock room. She heard his dismayed exclamation and dropped the broom.

The copier was off. Ainsley squeezed between it and its neighbor, peering behind. *No cord.* How was there no cord? The neighboring copier had one, plugged into a wall outlet. *Underneath?*

Ainsley knelt down before the machine. The copy center still glowed its after-hours green, and she realized she didn't know where that light came from. She looked around for a green exit sign, something. Nothing, but she saw the strange shadows moving on the wall above the copier. They looked like . . . branches, leaves, ruffled by an unseen wind. They were ephemeral, there for a second, then gone, then back again, shyly. She stared at them as if hypnotized. What had she hoped to feel, upon finding a miracle? She felt . . . hard and clear and empty, a perfect crystal vessel waiting to be filled, as she looked under the machine.

There was a cord! No, there were many cords, a tangled skein of cords coming out of the bottom of the machine. They weren't plugged in to anything, instead they had forced their way into the floor, through the industrial carpet and down into a network of cracks in the concrete. The machine started its purr. Another piece of white paper emerged. Trembling, still on the floor, Ainsley retrieved it.

We used to be so tall, you can't even imagine.

Stuffed Shark Puppet by Adrienne Celt

No one wants to be remembered for only their worst day, but what I'm suggesting is that it's equally bad to be remembered for your best. For me that was the day of the carnival, which started with Cheerios drowning in blue skim milk and ended in this, a toy from the midway. The toy we all wanted, and had been trying to win for years. It took a hundred tickets.

It's a nice shark, about 20 inches long, and the puppet mouth is functional. I washed it a couple of times, and air dried it, so the thing is perfectly clean. A hundred tickets was the equivalent of winning fifty games of Skee-Ball, but of course my brother and I had rules about playing every single booth. You couldn't just do Skee-Ball, you had to pop the balloons in the mouths of the devil clowns and do the ring toss into the bowls of goldfish and use the BB gun to shoot the metal ducks every time they popped up against the wooden forest in the background. I still remember that *ting* when you made the shot, because I was a terrible at that game, and I almost always missed.

Some days you just win, though. Some days you can't lose. We ate Cheerios at home because we wanted to save all our money for the carnival. First we had to ride the Zipper, which of course is a death trap, and then we had to eat a funnel cake, and then we had to spend the rest of the day, until closing, on the games.

The way I felt about those games is the way I feel now about building a functional boat: it's a nice dream, an almost plausible challenge, but one that's actually insurmountable when you take into account the realities of my life. Sure, I could learn proper woodwork. Take a class, read a book, apprentice with a master craftsman. It's not like I can't imagine the steps I would have to follow. But I won't. So I fuck around in my garage with an old wooden rowboat I got on Facebook Marketplace, drinking beers and listening to podcasts while I sand it down. What with the kids, my job, occasionally wanting to hang out with my wife, I have about an hour to spend that way every week.

I didn't need the games to be anything different. They were the fire that lived inside me three hundred and sixty four days of the year. Jack and I spent hours talking strategy, trying to decide the best order of operations, which Skee-Ball machine was the one with the sensitive 500-level ring so you could get the points even if your ball didn't make it in. Whether they might fix that. Who would be running the booths. Would Shirley be there: Shirley with her crop top, and her bright red curly hair. She was thirty years old, but she seemed ancient to us, like an incredibly sexual witch. Talking about the games was always better than playing the games: playing was where life let you down. But that was okay, because you had the rest of the year to talk.

So on the day of the carnival, it was a surprise when I started making my shots. "Whoah, Andy," Jack said, when I hit my third clown. I can still hear the waver in his voice. Impressed with me, maybe for the first time. He and his friends started out by trying to beat me, but it was a lucky streak like none of us had ever seen, and in the end they just followed me from booth to booth as I racked up my wins.

The carnival comes through town in late spring, when it's finally light out later in the evening, and all that light is golden. Have you ever had a fully golden day? When the blood running through you is also that same color, and it shimmers, and you know you can do no wrong? I thought, *This is it.* That my life was beginning. That all the moments leading up to that day, with the Skee-Ball spinning off my fingers, the ring tossing effortlessly onto the hook, had been my preparation. Something that starts like this can't stop, can it? It can't just be all the luck of your life rolled into three hours on the midway. Can it?

I don't mean to say I've had a bad life. It's been a pretty regular one. Sometimes my hard work pays off, and sometimes it doesn't. I just thought that once I found that golden feeling, I'd be able to get it back. And that hasn't been my experience.

This shark has been sitting on my dresser for years, and I finally decided that it's not reminding me of anything good. I thought it was a secret signal of the things that were to come. But now I feel like it's getting in the way of me really living my actual life.

It would be a good toy for a little kid. I never let mine play with it, and now they're too big. But maybe you won't miss that moment. Maybe this luck is for you.

Symbol of Sailing and Memories (Porthole Painting) by Ryan Daniels

At midnight, rain was pouring heavily and flooding the roads. Two friends went inside for shelter and to stay for the night. "Thanks for letting me stay at your place for tonight," Aaron said.

Jake responded, "You're welcome. Didn't expect the storm to hit as heavily with the ocean tides rushing heavily out there. You are free to stay here overnight, or if the storm slows down, you can head out if you wish to."

"Thanks, but I will see where things are at with me and the storm, especially us having a couple beers together," Aaron said.

Jake looked around, admiring Aaron's place. "Love the house, nice interior, and like the decorations on the shelves and walls. All the Hawaiian tropical themes to fit where we live after all." Jake then noticed an unusual decoration, a sailboat cruising in the open ocean, printed within a circular plastic-metal looking design.

The decoration looked like something you would see at a fisherman's wharf in California. Or like something you put out as a decoration in a bathroom rather than being out on a living room wall. "Why do you have this on your wall?" Jake asked.

Aaron looked at the object, smiled, and said. "Oh, it's something from a past life I had before I ended up here. Look at it often to bring back good memories. The image represents to me the adventure of exploring the open ocean and experiencing the world, as we only have one lifetime. Back in the days when I was with my brother, Caleb, on our father's sailboat, my father called the boat, Besie. Caleb and I called it The Codfather. Inspired by one of our favorite classic movies. Cruising through the Pacific and exploring the open world, and letting the ocean take us to where next."

"I never knew you had a boat," Jake said.

"Yep, after Caleb and I graduated from high school, our father always wanted us to explore this planet as it has to offer. He gifted us the boat, and we took off from our hometown in San Clemente, California, to set sail to the unknown, but we had a map, which we decided to follow in the direction of the Pacific Ocean. Going to new lands, especially when the sunsets are always the best to experience, and when finding an island, you see the cities or towns come alive with the lights in buildings, homes, beaches, and forest areas. Showing the signs of life and the adventures that we both would find by heading there every time, along with the adventure of being out in the water."

Aaron continued, "The ocean will always have its moments, getting the nice cool ocean mist spray, seeing seagulls soaring over the ocean, and coming across multiple ocean life besides catching small fish for endless cheap meals. Finding whales, dolphins, sharks, turtles, sting rays, and many more. You see everything out in the ocean, the good and the bad. It takes a lot of responsibility to keep The Codfather in good shape, always docking at an island and stocking up on supplies and new sails in case one rips. Fresh filtered water rather than getting sick from the salt ocean water, and more importantly, any storms that come through with rain, lightning, and rough waves that make it hard to control the ship."

Aaron started laughing, "Another issue was my brother, sometimes he would be a pain in my ass, but I still love him. I took more control of the ship while he was focused on the experience. He would help, but not as much as he would, and would curse a lot. With sailors having multiple naughty words they can say without penalty. I would say we were sailing together for at least a couple of years."

"What happened to The Codfather?" Jake asked.

Aaron answered, "Well, unfortunately, in life you sometimes have to make some tough decisions, and sometimes it's a sacrifice, and that I found was more important than exploring the ocean."

"What is that?" Jake asked.

"I found love," Aaron replied.

"Aw, how sweet," Jake said.

Aaron responded, "Yeah. During the exploration, I met a wonderful girl, and she meant a lot to me. Her name was Andrea, and I met her here in Hawaii, and eventually I had something more than a boat to look after and had a little daughter named Eli."

"Had? How come I have never known you had a wife and daughter? I have known you, man, for a while now," Jake asked.

Aaron answers, "Another sacrifice hit, and things didn't last long between Andrea and me, after the divorce papers were complete. We both chose what was best for our little girl, and that I would take care of her on selected days each week while she did the same on her end. Sacrifices have to be made sometimes, and I do miss my old life on the ocean and having a family, but I don't regret any of my choices, especially the gift that was my daughter."

Jake nodded and said, "That's good."

Aaron continued, "As for The Codfather, once I met Andrea, Caleb took over control of the boat, and at first, he felt sad and stressed about being alone, but he wanted to continue to see this open world and was willing to make that choice as well. Even though the responsibilities weren't really there with him before. Six months after he left, he came back to Hawaii, and The Codfather was heavily damaged. Caleb told me it was from multiple storm damages, and it would have been costly to repair. The sails were ripped, and the boat was filthy. Since the boat was for both of us, Caleb knew at least how to drive the sailboat. I trusted that he would be able to go out on his own, but I was wrong. Our dad was for sure upset and disappointed, but didn't want to hate Caleb or me because of the boat, though. The Codfather had to be sold for parts, and I kept a window frame as a token of the memory of The Codfather, which is the frame on the wall. Went to a local artist store and had them print a cheap sailboat in the open heavy tide ocean, seagulls flying, and a light sunset background to put into the window frame. In total only cost me $5.00, compared to if we fixed The Codfather. Which would have cost $3,000. Being on The Codfather made me feel free and strong, like I could conquer the open world with the ocean being massive and areas that probably not everyone has explored. That was the exciting part about it, and I will never forget those memories, and that art piece decoration will always have a purpose to me, and I hope it will be for someone else."

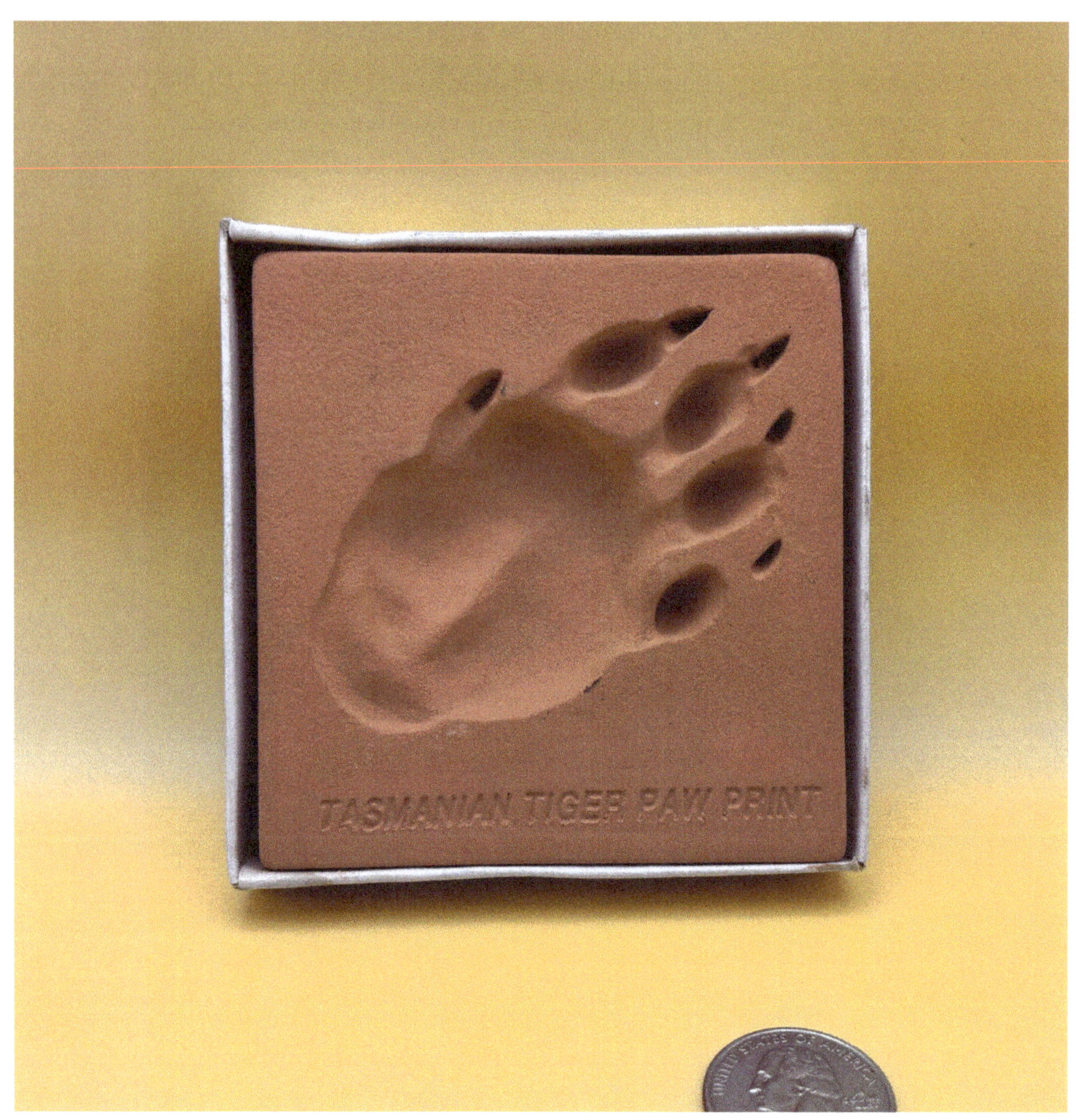
TASMANIAN TIGER PAW PRINT

Tasmanian Tiger Tile by Dana Diehl

"A Lasting Impression from Tasmania" costs $3.99 at the Tucson Goodwill on 22nd. In the center of the terracotta-red, clay tile is a neatly pressed pawprint. The words stamped neatly beneath it: TASMANIAN TIGER PAW PRINT.

When I flip the tile over, I find a sticker on the back that reads: "Thought to be extinct, many believe the Tiger (Thylacinus Cynocephalus) still roams the rugged wilderness of Tasmania [...] With the assistance of the Tasmanian Convention Bureau you can capture a stunning and unique venue for your next meeting or convention. One that will create a lasting impression and many happy memories."

I trace my fingers over the thylacine's pawprint. The digits leave little, round pools that might collect morning dew if left behind in the mud. The claws create deep wells.

The thylacines were officially declared extinct in 1982, though by that point about 50 years had passed without a confirmed sighting.

There are likely many causes of their extinction in Tasmania. Lack of genetic diversity. Distemper. A decline in prey. And, of course, the familiar story: the widespread, strategic slaughter of thylacines following European settlement in Tasmania. Though evidence shows that thylacines were more likely to hunt small and medium-sized prey, they quickly gained the reputation of killing farmers' sheep and were systematically hunted to the edge of extinction.

The sticker on the back on the plaque claims "an impression of an actual Tigers [sic] Paw ©." I wonder what that means. Did an actual thylacine touch this tile? Did someone sneak into a living thylacine's enclosure, gently press its paw into the wet clay? Or maybe the paw belonged to a thylacine already dead, stuffed, and housed in a natural history museum.

Most likely it's an impression of an impression. At some point, a mold was made of the thylacine's pawprint, and then that mold was used to mass produce souvenirs to draw businessmen to the Tasmanian Convention Bureau.

How many steps removed is this item from an actual, living thylacine?

It feels familiar, this pawprint. I have a similar one, sitting on my bookshelf.

After euthanizing my dog, Angie, in 2023, the vet clinic gave us a clay plaque with her pawprint pressed into it. My husband and I added it to the "Angie shrine" on our bookcase, where we also keep her collar, her ashes, and a small, crude sculpture I made of her when she was alive.

Angie's pawprint is almost the same size as the thylacine's. The thylacine's paw is narrower. The toes are more ovular, and there's a fifth digit kind of like a thumb.

Angie's pawprint is imperfect. It's not neatly centered on the plaque like the thylacine's paw; one of her nails presses over the edge. While the thylacine's print is perfectly smooth, Angie's prints are coral-textured, showing where the clay clung to her when they pulled her foot away, showing the roughness of her skin.

The vet clinic gave me Angie's pawprint when I picked up her ashes, about a week after her death. I remember not feeling as attached to this memorial as I expected to be. I felt closer to her collar, which still has bits of her fur clinging to it. The metal tags that would cling together and sometimes wake me in the night as she roamed the house in the dark. Her collar reminded me of her alive and warm and moving, while the empty pawprint reminds me of her absence.

I remember wondering, like I do now about the thylacine pawprint, how they made this impression. Did they do it when they briefly took her to a back room to place the catheter in her vein? Or did they do it after she'd already died, after we'd left the room and they wrapped her body in a blanket?

Once the thylacine trod through forests of myrtle, through high moorlands, eucalyptus leaves pressed under paws, rabbit bones cracked between teeth.

Decades after its extinction was declared official, the possibility that the thylacine is still alive, out there, in hiding, has been spun into something like an urban legend.

Online, you can find endless blog posts and Reddit threads from people claiming to have seen a thylacine. People sharing pictures of muddled pawprints in sand, pictures of scat next to measuring tape, asking other believers for help.

I can't find a single lab in Southern Australia willing to test this sample. Any leads?

Update: thanks for recommendation. Scat came back 93.5% wombat but don't wombats leave cube-shaped scats? Maybe thylacine ate wombat?

However, there are also arguments for the thylacine's continuing existence that feel more convincing.

In 2021, conservation biologist Barry Brook released his analysis of over 1,200 claimed sightings of the thylacine between 1910 and the present. He rated each sighting based on its likelihood of being accurate. How long did the individual observe the thylacine? How far away were they from the subject? Was it a professional witness with experience that made them more likely to correctly identify the creature?

Based on his investigation of the data, he believed that the thylacine was extinct, but most likely disappeared between 1990 and 2000, decades later than previously believed.

This—coupled with the fact that Tasmania is covered in vast, uninhabited wilderness with areas that are virtually inaccessible—makes it understandable that people can hold onto hope that the thylacine is still out there.

What makes the quest for extinct species so appealing? Why is it so tempting to hold onto the "maybe," to resist the evidence that something is truly gone?

Sure, you can say that it's for fun. It's like a treasure hunt. Though rare, there is a precedent for animals "coming back from the dead." They call these Lazarus species.

But I think there's more to it than that.

I think the search for the thylacine reflects a desire to assuage our guilt. If the thylacine is still out there, it means that, though humankind certainly hurt the thylacine, it didn't succeed in eradicating it.

When my dog died, the grief was paired with an overwhelming disorientation. Where had Angie gone? I saw her in every creature. "Is that you, Angie?" I'd ask the hummingbird that paused to assess me before zipping over to the feeder. "Is that you, Angie?" I'd say to the fly that wouldn't stop hovering around my face.

The thylacine isn't like the dinosaurs, which have only ever existed to us as fossils or puppets or CGI creatures on a big screen. Humans coexisted with thylacines for a while.

I watch a compilation of black and white videos of thylacines in captivity, pacing their small enclosures. Sniffing the air. Lying in a patch of warmth and, eyes closed, pointing their nose to the sun. The ridge of the thylacine's spine reminds me of the Catalina Mountains in Tucson, which I gaze at every day over my backyard wall.

Watching these videos makes me think of CAConrad's (Soma)tic Poetry ritual, "Resurrect Extinct Vibration." The ritual involves Conrad inducing a trance by lying on the earth and "saturating" their body with the recordings of recently extinct animals.

What does it mean when the world's tapestry of sound loses a thread? When we no longer have the barks and hisses and growls of a thylacine? One day, those sounds disappeared forever. With every extinction, the world becomes a quieter place. Though maybe quieter is the wrong word. Because in reality, the world is louder than ever—whale songs drowned out by the sound of naval sonar and shipping vessels and construction, the skies crowded with planes and the roar of highways.

The sound of the world isn't quieter, but it is flatter.

A Most Peculiar Wish (Avon Cologne Bottle) by Mackenzie Dougherty

Once upon a time, there was a tall and proud perfume bottle full of the most peculiar wishes…

It appeared on a clear-skied day in 1959. The dark glass caught the sun and bent it into bright hues of copper, its sharp edges of softening into an elegant and tall curve. It appeared well worn, chips of silver coating crumbling from the topper as if many a hand had once opened it. On a single frame of its body bloomed green leaves curling into read and yellow and pink petals, blue shadows of life flying around. No perfume lived inside the bottle, yet when it was opened, it released a scent that could not be a single name. It was romance intertwined with tragedy, joy cut thin with sorrow. It smelled of endings and beginnings.

On that particular morning, a factory worker found the bottle standing among rows of clear and amber perfume vessels, all identical, all full. This bottle stood taller, darker, prouder, as if it had chosen to rest differently than the rest. The man frowned. He twisted the bottle in his hands once, then twice. There was no label. Believing it to be a mistake, he slipped the peculiar bottle into his coat and carried it home.

That night, he set it on his nightstand, resolving to discard it in the morning. But his wife, who was always drawn to forgotten things, saw it. The moment her eyes landed upon the bottle, her breath hitched as though it had spoken her name without a sound.

"Give it to me!" she insisted.

"It's nothing, dear," her husband replied. "There is no perfume in it."

That night, long after her husband fell asleep, the woman sprung upright in bed with the bottle cupped in her petite hands. Moonlight spilled across the painted flowers. She twisted the silver top. The scent pulled her in, the air thickening. From the mouth of the bottle rose a thread of cloudy smoke of colors she could only see when she closed her eyes and dreamt.

The smoke bent and danced into a figure neither large nor small, young nor old. His form shimmered like heat on concrete, his eyes deep as stars in space. He bowed in a slow and solemn pace, as though stretching centuries of wait off his bones.

"I am the keeper of what is wished and lost," the being said. "I grant you three wishes."

The woman's heart thudded rapidly, "any three?"

The genie's face lowered into a mischievous grin, "any three, but head this, wishes are not created, they are borrowed."

The woman did not understand, but she nodded anyways. Her first wish came quickly, spoken with the ache of her years behind it. She wished for love to feel safe, for her marriage to be filled with warmth and ease, untouched by doubt or fear. In the days that followed, her home became a place of peace. Arguments from the husband dissolved into smiles and consideration.

The laughter became thin, however. The surprises that began, ended. Love that became protected from risk had also been protected from the depth of passion and craze. It became gentle, but distance, like a painting admired but never touched.

When the woman became bored of her first wish, she waited until her husband slept to open the genies bottle once more. For her second wish, she wished for beauty that would never fade. The genie warned, "Beauty preserved is beauty unmoving."

The woman's reflection remained young while many years passed unnoticed. Flowers in her garden never wilted, objects in her home never wore down. Nothing changed. Seasons blurred together without decay. Without endings, beginnings never came. People began to look at her strangely, time moving on without her. Her world became a bubble stuck in time, isolated from change.

Years had passed before the woman opened the peculiar bottle once again. On a random day, her husband, not effected by the wish of everlasting beauty, died sleeping in bed. Heartbroken, the woman could take it no longer. She pulled the bottle from her nightstand.

"I wish to return what was borrowed, please," the woman said softly, "I wish for things to change!"

The bottle trembled in her hands. The scent of romance and tragedy breathed once more. Time loosened its grip on the woman. Love regained its risk and beauty learned to age. As the genie began to depart, he sent her a wink and a small nod of his head. When the smoke faded, the bottle no longer rested in the woman's hand, but the warm hand of her husband. The woman was overjoyed.

Years later, when the woman was gone, the bottle appeared once more among the clear vessels of perfume in a factory, waiting patiently for another pair of hands and another heart willing to wish and dream and learn.

For such a peculiar bottle never disappears. It only waits.

Carving of Bacchus by Paul Ducker

This piece is a depiction of the Roman god Bacchus (or Dionysus for the Greek equivalent), god of wine and revelry. Some might wonder if the Greek or Roman gods play more significant roles in our modern lives, I would ask them to name the planets. This particular version is distinct from the early post-Renaissance depictions. Those most often were idealized sculptures, busts and statues. This one instead, presents a more realist and natural flow compared to the previous stylized and idealized versions. The idea of this stems from the later Enlightenment era artistic obsession with a realist interpretation of art. A few of these renditions were produced for a modern reenactment of Saturnalia, an ancient Roman holiday. During this day, the social norms would be flipped with masters being the ones to serve slaves and servants, social interactions being reversed. In addition, gifts would be exchanged and a great deal of wine would be consumed. The main deity of this titular holiday was Saturn, though with the crucial business of partying necessitating a substantial donation to the vineyards, Bacchus would also see significant "worship." This piece, along with the few others made for this set, were created for a modern reenactment hosted in Georgetown, Illinois. Though the town itself is tiny, it remained the major point of conglomeration for the "Classical Modern Discovery Society," due to its location between Springfield and Indianapolis (where the two sects of the society and most members resided).

The way they performed the reenactment was based on changing social norms, or pretending to invent old ones to do so. Typically, this was simply choosing some to be high society and others to be low society, and then reversing their roles as such. This was a biannual event for about a decade before it ceased, and part of that society was likewise terminated just a few years ago. This particular set of wood carvings of Bacchus was distributed during the last Saturnalia event. These were prizes that were given to a few members of the Springfield group. They had no idea it would be the last of such events and wouldn't find out until the next year. These prizes were given for performances in a rendition of an ancient play. Each sect of the society had its own group to compete against the others, and so minor prizes were given out, such as Bacchus here, to further the stakes a bit. Though in this case, these items would create a rift between the two sects and eventually the Classical Modern Discovery Society would be effectively dissolved.

It began a few months after this, well before the next reenactment of Saturnalia. A member of the Indianapolis sect, Jarold by name, bought a new brewery and recalled the sculpted Bacchus. He wanted to have one staring at him on the wall in his brewery. However, only 5 of these were made and those that made them were no longer operating, so getting new ones would have been difficult. These also held a special value to him since he quite enjoyed the society, though most of the Indianapolis sect, and all of the Springfield sect, didn't like the man (he was a real asshole usually). He did host the monthly meetings and many local events for the Indianapolis sect, as well as pay for most of the expenses they incurred. But he never let anyone forget it… He was actually the one to pay for the creation of these wooden Bacchi, though he specifically agreed that they would be used as prizes and he wouldn't claim any ownership over them. But he decided he wanted them anyway. Or at least one of them. He also had problems with relinquishing prizes after the fact with some of the previous ones he paid for. He bullied? (my source is unclear), the Indianapolis members into giving up one of the previous ones (a plastic gladius and Roman scutum shield). That is why they made him specify that he would not be able to do so this time. The other occurrence was at least at the event. But now, months later, he wanted them to bring it over from Springfield. Initially, he wanted them to drive all the way there instead of mailing it, but he later settled on mailing. One member who had a Bacchus said he was paying well over what he made in a day's pay, but he really didn't like the guy. He refused to sell it to them since he figured Jarold already got enough of what he wanted. The others were likewise refusing. They agreed that none would sell to him. This upset the little man, and he used what power he had to make the lives of the Indianapolis sect miserable. By cancelling meetings, rescheduling events to make sure they fit with no one's schedule, the Indianapolis sect soon lost half its members in a few months. Eventually they managed to get a new location and funding, but by then, there was little left of them, and they had been thoroughly demoralized. They did not attend the next biannual meet in Georgetown, and soon after, their sect died out. One of the Springfield members, who wishes to remain anonymous for fear of Jarold's head exploding, gave me his piece, specifically to sell to literally anyone but him. I can't say for sure if it was worth the dissolution of the Indianapolis sect. But I can say with the utmost confidence, that the eyes do not stare back at you when it is placed on a wall, unless you are drunk.

"BEST"
WHITE ELEPHANT
GIFT

Best White Elephant Gift Ever by Timothy Dyke

When I was thirty-six, I came out of the closet as gay. During that year, I fell into this unhealthy obsession with a straight twenty-three-year-old. He was addicted to cocaine and alcohol. To tell that story is to tell too many stories. He stole from me. He spit in my face once. I put up with his abuse because I thought I deserved it. I'm sure I abused him emotionally in return. The last time I ever saw him, we were standing in a field across from a mini mall in Escondido. He told me he wanted me to smoke crack with him. Just once. So I could feel what he felt. For some reason, he had this one-peso coin in his shirt pocket. He offered it to me. He said it would help me remember him. I turned down neither the pipe nor the peso. I carried that peso in my wallet for five years, long past the end of that twisted friendship. One Saturday morning in Honolulu, I was walking from my apartment in Makiki to the Barnes and Noble in Ala Moana Center. A homeless man asked me for money. Feeling something between generosity and obligation, I reached into my pocket and scooped out a handful of change. The peso must have slipped from my wallet. I accidentally gave it to the homeless man. It would have been meaningless to him. It had meaning for me. Just the other day, at the Goodwill across from the Honolulu Art Museum, I saw this little plastic trinket. Maybe it had been fastened to the top of a trophy once. It was marked with a saying: Best White Elephant Gift Ever. Just another useless thing I've brought into my life. I am a keeper of junk and ephemera, so desperate to find significance in the world that I imbue the meaningless with meaning. Useless objects are drawn to me. I keep them for a while until I sell them or lose them or give them away.

UNITED STATES OF AMERICA
LIBERTY
QUARTER DOLLAR

Gramma Christmas (Christmas Troll) by Megan Culhane Galbraith

Gramma Astrid passed away on Christmas Day three years ago. The family grieved for months. We'd lost our matriarch. We missed her Sunday soup suppers and her sharp tongue. We missed her stories most of all. She was our bridge to the past.

The great grands marveled at her tales of excitement seeing the first passenger trains rumble into Brattleboro VT, and they loved how she tucked them in under the old electric blankets in the unheated upstairs of her Vermont home. Astrid was 102 and had lived in South Newfane her entire life. Her home was a rambling Colonial with a wagon wheel light fixture in the living room and a piano for banging on. PopPop's hunting rifle hung over the fireplace, and the sprawling attic contained what felt like miles of treasures. The kids called the winding upstairs halls "secret passageways."

Her caretaker, Romeo, lived in the back apartment like a houseguest. We only saw him when he shoveled the driveway or mowed the lawn. He died years before she did, probably from smoking so much.

Her hair had been jet black, long, and lush in the early photos she kept by her bed. The beauty shop in town styled Gram's white hair high, and teased it up into the pony tails she wore as a teenager. She'd said it was to cover a bald spot at the crown of her head that had grown slowly larger with age. She had a collection of colorful wide satin ribbons, and tied her hair like she was wrapping a gift.

When she passed away, my youngest daughter, Delia, found this troll doll at a junk shop and named her "Gamma Christmas." She carried that little doll with her for a year, massaging its soft white lamb hair between her right thumb and forefinger while sucking her left thumb. When two front teeth pushed their way through her pink gums, that was the end of the thumb sucking and "Gamma Christmas" was consigned to her jewelry box with the dancing ballerina.

Later, we hot-glued a small pin to the doll's back so Delia could wear it on the lapel of her school uniform at Christmas-time.

Welcome

You've Been Gnome (Gnome Figurine) by Yadira Garcia Soto

Gnomes keep many secrets in their little hats.

From their innocent welcome signs and their little blue birds, everything about them screams secrets. They are a farce, creatures who think themselves better than fairies, beings who like to be in gardens for their own convenience. Never be deceived by gnomes; they are the sacred enemies of humans. They keep lies and secrets, demonic creatures in our gardens, watching us walk to our cars while they pretend to protect our homes. It's a scam, a deception hidden beneath their rubber shoes. They exist for one reason: to spy on us and dominate the humans one day, after an epic war against squirrels and ceramic. It's their right, after what humans have done.

They created the art of espionage, and then improved it as the art of defense against dogs. Gnomic lessons are methodical; only the toughest survive the teaching, and only the best emerge unscathed. They don't protect us, but they watch us. They have deceived us with their propaganda. We are enormous beings compared to them, but they keep secrets, secret weapons behind their hats. They have a society where they sell themselves at low prices wholesale, one gnome for every house. Their headquarters and houses are located in these factories; no health inspector has ever left alive. They have the best gnomes learning marketing so they can sell their fellow gnomes to more humans every day. That was the training, their way of life, accounting books with flower drawings. The ultimate goal of this business is to have every human house surrounded by gnomes, small armies strategically positioned to attack us. Every cookie spent on the education of each gnome is a cookie well spent.

Dirty, secretive ones who remain motionless, observing us as if they were better than us. They know they are better, that they can dominate us. They just need to multiply; humans won't be able to fight thousands of gnomes at once. They've seen it in ants, their ancestral animals. Thousands can dominate a single. Humans find them everywhere, every Dollar Store and Home Depot, pretending to be adorable when they are unknown beings. They know what we think of them, secretly mocking humans. How adorable are the ignorant humans, buying gnomes as if they were toys. The perfect scam.

Each gnome is a hidden warrior, guarding the secrets and traumas of ancient gnome wars beneath their beards. Battles filled with pottery, stabbed dogs, and resource-stealing squirrels. Let's not even talk about the war against the Christmas elves in '48. So much death, so much blood, gnomes know how to fight. They create programs to train new generations, demonstrating the easiest ways to deceive humans, their final enemy. The rules are simple:

Any gnome must appear innocent, the epitome of fragility. Otherwise, they must hide their faces under hats and fake beards; humans must not suspect a thing. Their faces should show the most feigned excessive kindness, and eyes as fragile as drops. They have to be, otherwise no one would buy them. Nobody likes an ugly gnome; they find them disgusting. That's why the ugliest gnomes now work in marketing. Rejection has made them fiercer; the more horrible they are, the more likely they are to become a CEO.

That's why adorableness is a sign of success in the home. The more adorable they are, the more easily they'll be bought. Capitalize on the cuteness explosion, use it to their advantage. However, the training isn't just about looks; it covers other aspects of domination. Gnomes are taught in gentleness, an innate aspect of their culture. Their ridiculous clothes are meant to throw us off. The art of disguise is second nature to them. Who would be afraid of a pointy hat like those Christmas elves and blue clothes like togas? Nobody. We're easy to fool. Flowers and little birds improve the image; everyone trusts flowers.

I know all of this because of a specific gnome—one I bought for its cuteness, but which has now become the very source of my undoing. I hear him at night through my security cameras. He knows I'm listening, but he enjoys watching me suffer, knowing that no one will believe me.

This gnome is the perfect spy, the ideal decoration for tulips. He had a name, one selected after years of discussion and recommendations from the other ugly gnomes in marketing. He chose an epic name, one that would be shouted in battles and praised in Gregorian chants, a name taken from the pharmacy section, popular these days.

Ozempic the Omnipotent, who will inject his victims and spill the lower blood.

He had years of training in the mystical arts of stoicism, to be sold and placed in a house. The gnomic revolution will come; Ozempic just has to wait. Patience is a virtue, and he had to learn it as if it meant floating. Aspirin, the Unbreakable, would be proud of him right now, so many years since that first lesson. This gnome hasn't broken his spying position since he arrived. He only whispers in strange dialects—ones I had to translate to discover the horror I had brought into my home. He knows that I know, and he looks at me with his hidden eyes in a petulant manner.

Ozempic just had to wait more; he will be part of the great revenge. The most legendary battle in history. His teammates, named after medications, will shout in victory alongside him, weeping over their new ruling. They will regain their birthright.

Gnomes lost their right to the land, condemned in the ceramics, a curse from jealous humans. A magnificent injustice, leaving them trapped in skins of glass, but that's their advantage now; nobody knows the risk of the glass now. It's the history Adderall the All Knowing has shown them, a tragedy as big as their fake hats. They must take revenge, show humans why they have such striking names. Gnomes will recover what they lost, no matter how many cuts they have to make. Their species is better than ours; they don't need dirty tricks to beat us. Ozempic sees it every day, useless humans glued to cell phone screens. This gnome just has to wait for the pecking war. Little by little, one gnome per house is a gnome victory for all.

Anyone who buys Ozempic risks being spied on, a future victim of this great warrior, watched in every move until the enemy becomes his most hated friend. He will know everything about you, even things you don't know about yourself. It is a perverse creature that only makes itself known when it sures that no one will believe the victim. There will be no peace in your nights, and your days will be pure paranoia. He will see you from the window and from the rose-filled patio. When Judgment Day arrives, all his accumulated rage will turn against you, no matter how many times you brush it off. The first enemy to defeat will be your pet, the creature that pees on him. The war against pets was the first lesson learned from Benadryl the Lich. One of the greatest warriors in modern history, who was recently defeated by a lawnmower. Then, it will go for what hurts the most, hitting your little toe with the force of a squirrel. Small but powerful pains. An insatiable warrior, with a sign that all are welcome. That's the gnome looking at you in the photo.

He has a favorite attack strategy for when the Day of Gnomish Domination arrives. He will call upon his closest allies, other gnomes who have hidden near your home, ready to dominate you with tacks. Nyquil of the Eternal Slumber, specifically, will prick your eyes while Xanax the Wise tries to drown you with vases of lemonade. Those two are great fighters, fierce with the scars of kids who kicked them. Ozempic, of course, won't be left behind while hitting you with plastic bags and flowerpots. Don't forget the marketing gnomes; now that they're free from their stinking offices, they'll attack the humans who rejected them. The most important marketing gnome, the CEO of all pottery, Tramadol the Tyrannical, will bite every human who rejected him years ago. He's, at the end, Ozempic's cousin. It will bite your fingers just for the sweetness of it. All the gnomes will win and dance in the blood of the pets. That will be my future if I stay with that bloodthirsty warrior. It must be someone else's problem.

Buy Ozempic, the Omnipotent, at your own risk.

SCHIRMER'S
WIRE BOUND
MANUSCRIPT
MUSIC WRITING BOOK
No.105
X-TRA
NAME
ADDRESS
CITY
STATE
ZIP
12 STAVES
9 x 12 UPRIGHT
96 PAGES

Unfinished Music Notebook by Mahsel Gatan

Arji couldn't time travel so of course he ended up trying other means of temporal trickery. One of the most unsuccessful of which happened to be this notebook.

He wanted to at least attempt to channel his meagre gift of foresight into something more tangible. If he could *just* pluck a song from the head of someone gifted with songwriting, he could release it before them and rake in passive revenue from its destined popularity. It turned out that the mental fortitude he had for seeing past The March of Time didn't extend into memorizing things well. Or comprehending them, really.

Writing down music came out a lot harder than those silly dots and stems made it seem. Arji tried real hard to copy down those written sounds from the glimpse he got from a celebrity ghost writer's journal! As soon as he had shown a friend with actual ability to read notes however, they'd laughed at him. It was unfortunate. It was even more unfortunate that he had prefaced "his" piece as being emotionally important to him. He had thought maybe it would have added extra empathy points to the story people would have circulated if he was famous and seemingly untouchable. Stuff like that really grounded a celebrity in memory, after all.

It was such a promising vision as well! He thought he glimpsed a few framed posters of various famous blonde singers in Taxi's peripherals. He liked to call the unbeknownst hosts of his divination perspectives Taxis. He wasn't driving, but he got to see the sights, so to speak.

It was an entire studio built into a multi-storied building with card scanners for entry. Whoever he had been in that future must have been quite renowned in at least the producing scene.

The music he tried to swipe had been on both paper and on a screen. There was a real desk, the kind that seemed fitted for the exact dimensions of the wall. It was slotted into place like counters in a kitchen. They were cooking up something, Arji just didn't know exactly what those ingredients were. He couldn't read the ingredients as well, apparently.

And on one of the lower tables next to a couch—there were couches! White couches, at that—there were those orange prescription medicine containers. The words on the labels were scribbled out, unreadable even as Taxi unscrewed one open and took two tiny round and white powder-pressed pills. He hated when he saw glimpses like this one, because as soon as things like medicine were addressed, the vision made reasons for those medicines to be known. At Taxi's swallow, pain at Arji's temple throbbed through. He hated sharing the symptoms, even if they were always temporary.

Taxi moved towards that fancy desk and it was there that Arji was given the rare sight of a divination perspective's reflection. Reflected in the black screen was dark, straight hair cut off at the chin. Her nose was wide but had a high bridge, evidenced by the screen even seeing that depth. He could also see shadows of eyebags creasing under her lower eyelids. She was nobody he recognized. It's not like Arji ever knows the people in his visions.

He watched through her tired eyes as she pushed the notebook with neatly jotted music notation to the side as she reached for the computer mouse. This was where things got tricky, Arji only knew of computers at all because his cousin had gotten one of those new things from work.

He had gotten plenty of looks at computers before from previous scrying, but it was always a gamble whether the computer would be something recognizably box-like or if it was going to be something impossibly thin and crisp. Arji had made the mistake of trying to acquire stock of a company sharing names or logos of those electronics before, but he didn't really have the money or credibility to invest in the first place.

She loaded it up, and it was one of those freaky types of screens that looked like a window into some alternate universe. Maybe it's a type of uncanny valley that Arji is just too dumb to comprehend yet, but it just seems wrong for a screen to be able to look like a window into the middle of the ocean or some beautifully dune-scalloped desert.

Then the illusions are broken by some sign in a box that takes it even deeper into a different world. The background changed into some movie still, and the actors in the scene are so crisp they look like they might move.

Taxi opened up a program that looks like a spreadsheet but greyed down and framed with virtual buttons and knobs that her cursor can interact with. It might as well be hologram work. When she clicked out of a spreadsheet with various colored rectangles into one that Arji can recognize for a score notation, he willed his real body to start moving the pen in his hand. He had positioned it there before immersing himself into the future, he made sure the ballpoint tip of it was placed on the middle line of one of the staffs.

She clicked some button and a blue line down the notation started moving across them, lighting up the notes and presumably playing them out loud. That was another caveat to his ability. Arji could only see into the future, not hear it. She just sat there, watching it pass by until it repeated itself twice and thrice. It was good, he had a good look at the placement of the notes and was able to scribble them down as best he could without his eyes active in the present.

Taxi paused the line suddenly, tapping so hard down on the left mouse button that Arji could feel a sting at his fingertip. Her cursor hovered over the notation sporadically, clicking and dragging notes and symbols around. The movement was strangely unsteady, like her wrist was twitching and flicking the cursor about in a way she ultimately gave up correcting. There was, is something that scrapes itchily under their palms.

They use the back of their hands to wipe at their face, and their vision is temporarily obscured by both their hands' solidity as well as their head's aching, icicle crash of hurt. They're forcing their hands back onto the keyboard and mouse, away from their face. Their fingers stretch, piano-trained, into pressing down multiple keys at the same time. It makes notes on the screen disappear, makes scribbles on the notebook dig themselves into the page.

There's a stinging cold sensation in their bottom lip and it warms along the edges as they force themselves to stop biting down hard enough to bleed. Their wrists hurt, some kind of carpal tunnel assisted angrily by itchy, wriggling bubbles burrowing thick in the veins flowing into their palms. They hiss, and their mouse flinches into pressing play.

There are big clusters of notes in different parts of the screen now, clinging together like grapes that will explode if they touch the other clusters. The big gaps between these notes are long, the blue line cutting down the screen moving over the staffs like a rake over bowling pins. There's a clatter in their vision when they catch onto the clusters just like pins too, blue lighting up the symbols and notes like tumors in an annotated screening. They had one of those, one of them did. If they shut their eyes now, their vision will jump into a future ahead of him and a past behind her into a white room with a paper-covered bed. They've seen x-rays before.

They keep their eyes open to the now? And there's black spots on the screen that stretch off of it. Technology is amazing in that way. They're black holograms everywhere, splotches of it with feathered edges the color of the world around them, blended like water spilled over grits of shattered watercolors. Their heads lolls forward, and the inkspots floating about drag down with their vision like nails on a chalkboard. And the nails are theirs, catching on nothing and straining in needled and pulled pain like their fingertips will split from the nailbeds.

The backs of their necks ache at the weight of their skulls trying to tumble off their torsos. Their torsos follow, slumping forward and making their wheeled chair slide back a step. A wheel clips on itself and then releases, making the chair slide back fast and slippery. When they fall off the chair, it's hard and sudden and right into the edge of the pretty, fitted, and neat desk.

Their forehead slams across the blue line of it, blue because of the tumors glowing off of the screen. It feels like something splits open, separating and dividing like rhythms cut up by engineered settings automatically splicing them into perfection. The black is everywhere.

Arji shocks into his body and present time with a shiver. Their notebook is on the table, and his hand is still holding the pencil. He can't read the music, but it has to mean something.

That means it must be worth something, too.

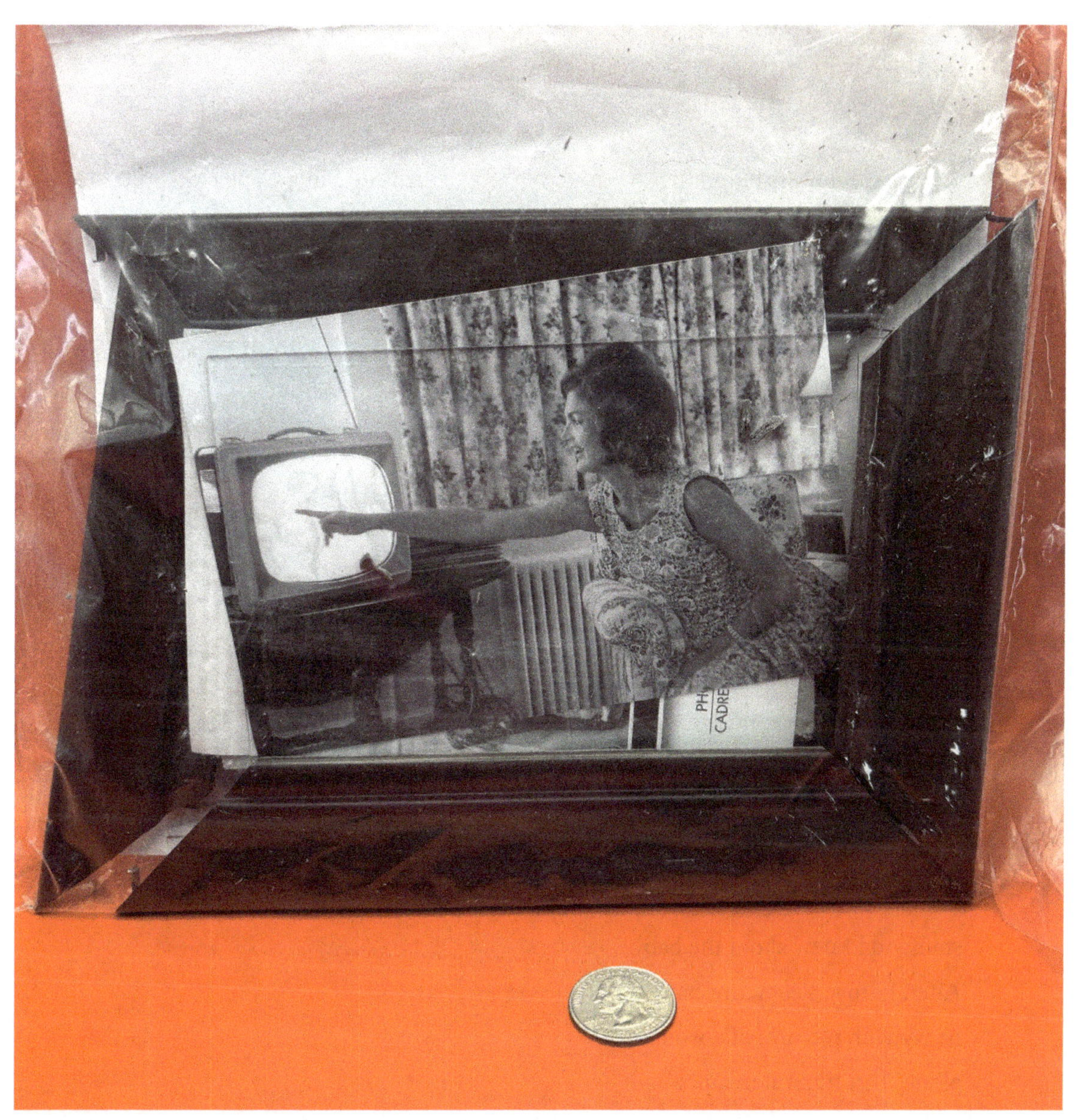

I Shot Jackie Kennedy (Photograph of Jacqueline Kennedy Onassis in a Broken Frame) by Avery Gregurich

There were flowers blooming everywhere. We sat quiet in the living room. It was still early out in Los Angeles. We watched Jack stand and speak to people who wanted him as their president. Little Caroline slept on the couch beside me. "There he is," Jackie said, and touched the TV. I lifted up my camera. Jackie said "Hell, Ted. Let me put out my cigarette first." She had changed since the sun went down. We both knew that this was how it would be from now on. That she would have to share him with the world. Only the staff and I knew about the baby. After, I drove sleepy, my camera heavy with pictures of a woman alone. That night I dreamt about the future in a Cape Cod hotel. I saw many flowers bloom. Not many nights later, I sat in front of my own TV and reached out toward Dallas. "There she is," I said, petals of blood rising on her dress. I am selling this photo, this broken promise. Please let me know if they break the frame.

Magnifying Glass* by Valyntina Grenier

The light doesn't work
So I focus my heart.
I see my precious mother
Living her best self
In a cold room in ill health.

We are of a world made up
By thieves, usurpers,
Warmongering men,
With no limits on violence
And degradation.

The Files! The DHS!
[insert list of atrocities here]
Gaza! Iran! On and back…
We can see the great grift
Of this administration; only hope

We may be flush with peace
And safety among each other
In our precious outdoors.
Desire joy and exercise. Look-
Behind some blackberry vines

A bird I can't identify
Looking just fine.

*Batteries not included. I purchased the object and wrote a poem before considering the implications of mailing something battery operated. As I'd hoped I was able to use new batteries and power the light. However, in the process of opening it I broke the piece that is meant to allow for opening and closing the battery compartment. Unfortunately, it was stuck shut by a corroded battery that expanded inside. Fortunately, I was able to clean it up and, as I said, get it working. The handle is currently closed with tape.

The Gospel of Captain Gentoo (Pirate Penguin Figurine) by Danielle Hartshorn

When you bump into a foldable table like an absolute doofus at the church-hosted garage sale, some 50-cent trinket is gonna fall on the concrete driveway and chip its swashbuckling hat, leaving you guilty as hell and holding a new, never *ever* needed in one's lifetime, penguin pirate figure. That's what happened to me. Apparently, it was God's plan for me to own a cheesy little cheapo trinket. Figures.

Anyway, it looked like one of those Gentoo penguins on the NatGeo channel. Every time I went to sleep nursing a sweaty beer on the La-Z-Boy, I swear I'd always find my way to tragic nature documentaries—the penguin kind. You'd see these little innocent babies waddling from their eggs just to get mauled by leopard seals twenty minutes later. Just there and gone, and *c'est la vie.* At least *this* 50-cent penguin cut a dapper figure: white poet shirt, billowy green pants, sashed cutlass, all while standing gloriously on a treasure chest. Its flowing human locks of hair and beak beard were a touch weird, I admit, but God be damned, it started to grow on me.

Plundering my high cholesterol heart.

So I rinsed the dust from the garage sale penguin and plopped it in the center of my freshwater tank as soon as I got home. After doing so, my hand started to tingle—pricks and needles and all that. And boy, did *it* start to feel right at home, comfortably tucked and enshrined in a bed of black aquarium gravel, its treasure booty covertly hidden by the thick anubias nana leaves and sword-shaped java ferns. It seemed to stand almost wistfully, like its beak was facing some heavenly horizon and not the filtration system gurgling away. My honey gouramis were wary of the new penguin, of course. They'd float about in the corners of the tank and mind their own fishy business, hiding under large algae-covered stacked rocks, eating flakes, and shitting on the gravel, but they'd always make it a point to avoid the center of the tank. Eventually, they started to get bolder. They'd get real close to the pirate penguin and stare with their goofy little eyes all inquisitive like. Just some fish mindlessly checking out a new tacky decoration in the tank.

But it became a bit freaky after that. My horde of orange fish began to nudge small pebbles to the penguin's plastic webbed feet. Always a specific kind of pebble: round and shiny and bulbous—like an eye. After they produced these precious offerings, they'd just gather around the penguin and stare. Just stare until they'd get tired and hover in place above the gravel, as if their duty to the statue was finished for the day. You'd think I'd be pulling your leg, but this ritual lasted for a while. I don't know if they ever slept. They wouldn't hide under rocks. They wouldn't eat their flakes. And they wouldn't shit. I would try to move them with my net to the far reaches of the tank, just to give them some time away from the penguin, but they would always wriggle out of the mesh and race back to the figure—violently twitching their fins, spasming, and hurling themselves toward the penguin just to *look* at it again, sometimes even bring another stupid pebble. By the end of the month, a little pyramid of gravel had formed around the penguin, making the figure rise and rise above them all. A true Christ the Redeemer statue look-alike.

I mean, I'm a normal person. I don't believe in God, for one. But from what I could see, these fish had something pretty damn close to Him. The fish's prayers rode on the artificially circulated currents of the tank. Their gospel floated in the bubbles coming from their open and closed devotee-fish mouths. And I even started to think that the penguin was holy—you know, with it having come from a church garage sale and all that. I thought that maybe a true sacred relic can instill faith even in the hearts of honey gouramis. A penguin priced by Father Martin himself. How was I supposed to know? I wasn't really a believer. All I really knew was that penguins ate fish.

But time went on, and I soon found myself in the habit of staring at the penguin, eyeing the God that presided over the tank. I ended up missing work on multiple occasions just to watch the soggy fish flakes dust the penguin's tricorne. See my fish kiss its webbed predator feet. You don't want to know how many calls I got from my boss—my gas station job almost went down the drain. And I don't know why I gazed at it, it wasn't as simple as this or that; seriously, who ever really knows *why?* I just wanted, and I felt, and so I did. Maybe the fish were like that, too. Maybe they hoped that they would finally understand if they looked hard enough in the penguin's darkly painted eyes. But I don't believe they ever *got* to know, because they eventually died off. One by one, I watched the bodies of my honey gouramis bloat and sprout lesions before they sank and littered the bottom of the tank. All six of the crew died in a circle around the penguin, eyes fixed on their maker. Going to their due reward seemed like. And after I fished their carcasses from the water, tossing them in the overflowing kitchen trash, I realized that I was all alone. My vision began to blur from the tears, but when I looked desperately at the statue, I could've sworn it was looking at me, too. Those paternal eyes holding all the kindness and goodness in the world.

For the first time since I was a little squirt sitting in the pews with my Grandma, I let my knees fall to the carpet, and I prayed. Blubbering and caressing the glass of the tank, I prayed for my pet fishes' pure, passionate spirits—those righteous gouramis following their pirate leader into fishy heaven.

Well, turns out low-quality paint leaks toxins into the water. Kills fish pretty easily.

Funny, right? But since *I* no longer have fish, *I* no longer need the figure.

After telling Father Martin the other day about all of this, we both decided that this penguin pirate gotta have its flock again. Fall into the next person's hands when they need it, because that's just what it does—you know, having a plan for each of us and all that. So I guess what I'm saying is that I hope it finds its home. Just not in a fish tank.

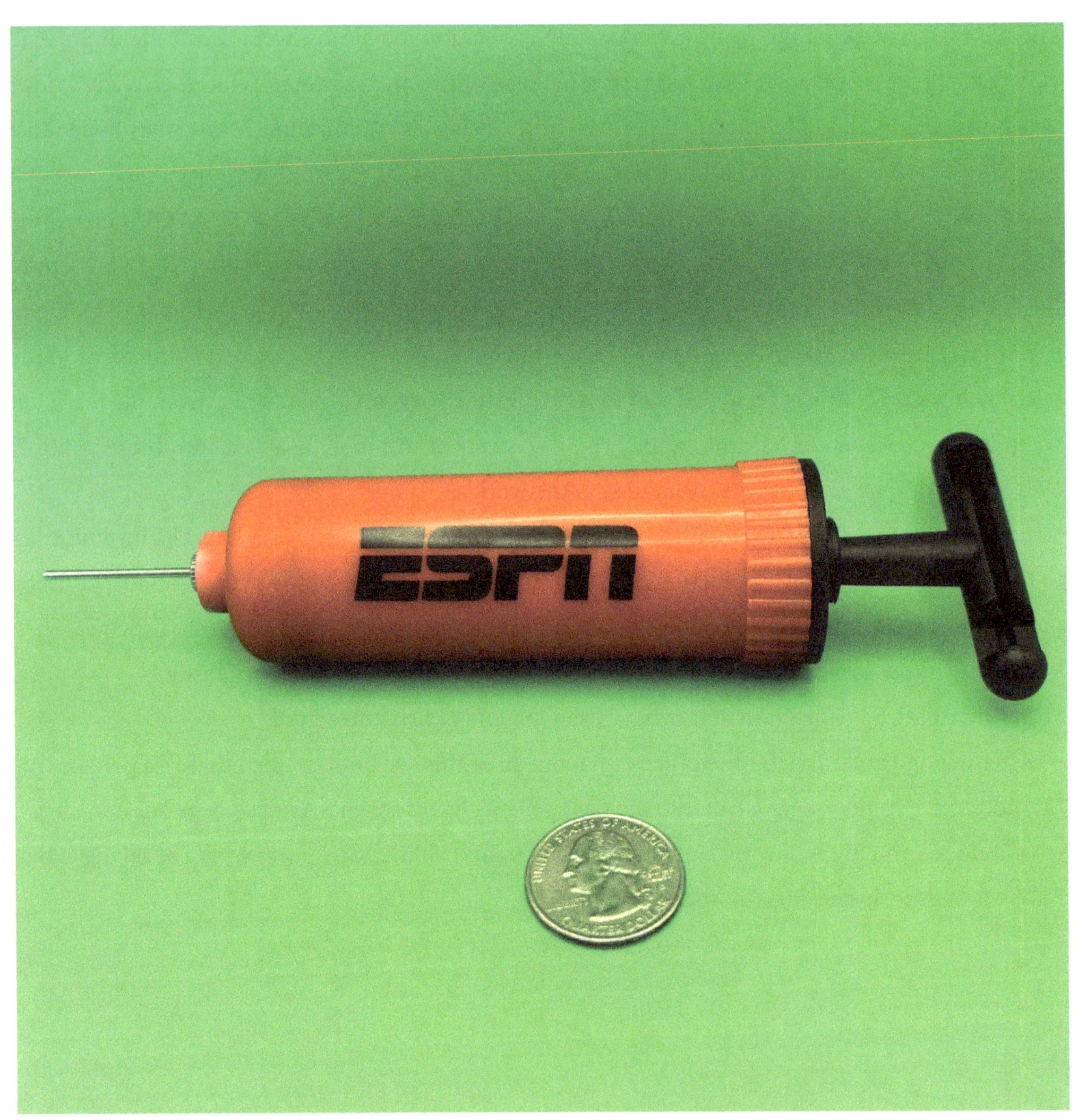
ESPN

My Pump (Mini-ESPN Hand Pump) by Wes Holtermann

After a long day digging graves for next to nothing, I drive to the Egg Palace on the freeway that skirts the glittering bay, under the Scarless Breast Augmentation billboard. The Opportunities College billboard. Then the Make Age Meaningless billboard, on which a man with a fake gray beard does pushups next to a bottle of supplements made from the powdered plasma of impoverished kids.

In the rearview mirror, the skin under my eyes has begun to sag. I'm no longer young. I'll start taking supplements. I'll get a job that pays. Start cooking for myself. But the neon Egg Palace sign buzzes forever in my future. They know me there. I'll order the eggs, as usual. It's always good to order what a place is known for. But I'll get a side salad too this time. I'm not getting any younger. I must improve myself.

Beside me, on the passenger seat, sits the small, red ball pump I bought months ago at the Goodwill. It's plastic. I was going to start playing again. I was going to change everything. Motion is lotion. But the basketball sits deflated in the closet. I never go in there. The closet is the exact dimensions of a grave. The ball is slumped like an old bulldog. Its skin is psoriatic and gray with disuse. The ball is me. It doesn't take a therapist. Still, I keep the pump beside me like a bible.

I didn't think I'd be digging graves into middle age. Ray calls the cemetery the hole factory. Another day, another hole, Ray says, lighting a cigarette. Sometimes we sit and watch the military salute, watch the crows startle at the gunshots and burst from the trees, listen to the rigid bugler play Taps as they lower the body, and then we go fill our hole right back up. Like nothing ever happened. Another waste of a day, Ray says, patting the soil flat with his shovel.

I drive on, past the pipes of the oil refinery. Now the Costco. The radioactive landfill that's become a dog park. The salt marsh cluttered with trash. The abandoned racetrack. Further on, another Make

Age Meaningless billboard. Same picture. Same supplements. On the radio, the Talking Heads singing something. Basically where's all my stuff.

There is no one on the road, and as I drive, I dream I'm pumping my mouth with the small red ball pump. I often dream while driving. In sleep, it's all still and black. On the road, I'm going somewhere. I insert the needle between my lips. The air tastes like ripe plastic. My mouth fills. My lungs. My skin begins to bloat prettily, gleamingly, moonlike. The creases around my eyes unwrinkle and engorge. In the dream I become plump, blemishless, shiny. I dream I'm a baby again, and it's a nice feeling.

A flock of pigeons shimmers under the overpass and crackles like fireworks. A veil of exhaust over the bay. Still beautiful. The defunct Chevy's on the water will soon be a Benihana, the sign says. Something to look forward to. I've never been, but it must be good. I've seen the commercials. Showmanship. Eggs in hats. The delight of the birthday boy. Wonder in the faces of men. Flames leaping from the grill. The Emeryville skyline on fire at sunset. I pump my mouth with my plastic pump and begin to sense I am on the verge of a great becoming. A great opening. Another day, another hole. Soon I'll be nothing but air.

F·R·I·E·N·D·S
THE TELEVISION SERIES
YOU'RE THE
MONICA
TO MY
RACHEL

Friends Themed Dog Toy by Caitlin Horrocks

My mother gave me this dog toy for my 30th birthday. It's the worst gift anyone's ever given me. This is a gift that makes grocery store flowers on Valentine's Day look like the Taj Mahal.

I do have a dog. Lola is an adopted pitty mix who's hard on toys. I can always use more. That's not the problem here. It's a set of three dog toys, printed nylon with squeakers inside: a palm-sized Monica, in a chef's outfit; a swoopy-haired Rachel, serving a cup of coffee; a rectangular gold frame containing the words, "You're the Monica to my Rachel."

I watched a few seasons of *Friends* when I was a kid. Sometimes with my mom, sometimes not. It was okay. I remember the characters in shorthand: "dim actor" or "awkward paleontologist." Had Ross really been a paleontologist? That made zero sense, but it made more sense than this dog toy.

"You're not like Rachel at all, Mom."

"Oh, I know."

"Am *I* the Rachel? You're not really a Monica either."

"Neither. They're for you to share with Lola."

Share? Like I'd chew on one myself?

"She's your Monica!" my mother announced enthusiastically.

"You think Lola is the Monica to my Rachel."

Our food arrived then, a turkey sandwich for me and a side salad for her because she didn't like to eat real food when people were watching. Seeing her stab individual shreds of carrot with her fork made me want to eat more, like I was proving something. My mother probably thought I was proving that I had no self-control. She'd asked if I could order the salad as my side and give it to her, so I could manage my portion size and she could save a few dollars, but I paid extra for the sweet potato fries because I had been dealing with this for officially 30 years now and I was tired.

"It's so sad what happened to Chandler," my mother said, maybe sensing that her gift was not a hit and trying to change the subject.

"What happened to Chandler?"

"You didn't see that he died? In a hot tub, but it was really drugs."

I was trying to imagine this episode, "The One Where Chandler Drowns in a Hot Tub," when it belatedly clicked that she was talking about the actor.

"My *dog* does not have an enormous rent-controlled apartment. My *dog* lives with *me*. I have a better job than Lola. I'm not, like, serving coffee while aspiring to work in fashion while she keeps us afloat."

Please note here that I can and do refer to my dog as a dog and not as a fur baby or fuzzy child or whatever. When it's just Lola and me, sometimes she's LilDroolyGobbleFace, but my mother does not know that. I am very happy with the current number of babies in my life, human or animal, and that number is zero. The number of romantic partners in my life is also currently zero and I'm not ecstatic about that, but I'm way more okay with it than my mother apparently is. She had no reason to define Lola as my ride or die, my soulmate, my best—

"You two are BFFs. That's what I meant."

"I have friends, Mom. Human friends."

"Of course you do," she said. "When did I say you didn't?" But she sounded like she was humoring a toddler who was insisting that their imaginary playground friends were real. I was seeing my human friends that night, for my birthday, I just hadn't invited her or let her know about it. The less information you give my mother, the less she has to weaponize, but the smaller she concludes your life must be.

"I was trying celebrate friends, friendship, you know, *Friends*," she said, pointing at the dog toy package. "Birthdays can bring up some challenging feelings around what we *don't* have, and I was trying to celebrate what you *do*."

My mother has never been to therapy but has read dozens of self-help books, none of which ever helped her help herself.

"So: what is it that you think I don't have?"

"Let's not do this," she said, like she was the mature one.

"Monica was a neat freak," I said. "Lola pukes on the rug when she eats too fast. Which a Monica would not do."

"She used to be fat."

"Lola?"

"Monica. In flashbacks."

My mother was probably mentally comparing my present size to Fat Monica, my past size to Thin Monica, a character arc in unacceptable reverse. "You think a *dog* is more put together than I am."

"Look, forget it, I don't know anything about dogs. Barry hated them. You know that."

My stepfather had indeed hated pets, even more than he disliked me and possibly my mother. I'd waited 20 years for her to leave him but instead he accidentally overdosed last winter and maybe it should have felt the same (she was free) but it didn't (she'd never freed herself).

"Wasn't there a character named Barry on *Friends?*" I asked. My stepfather had been he-who-must-not-be-named for most of my life, my own personal Voldemort, but the question floated past like a conversational life preserver and I grabbed it.

"He was the boyfriend Rachel doesn't marry. Leaving him at the altar kicks off the whole show. He's why she moves in with Monica in the first episode."

I hadn't remembered any of that.

"I rewatched the whole thing last spring," she said.

There was something sad here, something Phoebe might be able to name, or that Joey could make a gentle crack about, but then my mother pushed her little metal cup of salad dressing toward me and said, "Do *you* want this? I shouldn't." And fuck that, fuck this gift that's dumb and mean but also depressing and I don't want it, I'll buy Lola some stuffed animals from the Goodwill to disembowel and someone please get this thing out of here.

Plastic Dinosaurs by Reed Karaim

I have known plastic dinosaurs who frolicked in the grass behind the Dublin Castle, who went to Hogwarts with Harry Potter, who had a passing friendship with Jeff Bridges. I have known plastic dinosaurs who were heroes and those who were afraid. I have known plastic dinosaurs who dreamed of greater or more terrifying things in their restless nights, as we all do. They have lifted me up and let me down, but for every plastic dinosaur I have known, I can say this: their hearts were always pure.

I can tell you when I first came to know plastic dinosaurs. It was one of those times, like ours, when the world was going to hell. The United States had invaded Iraq for what would turn out to be false reasons and people across Europe were horrified. There were mass protests against the war. We were living for part of the summer in Dublin and writing, after we dropped our four-year-old daughter off at daycare, in the reading room of the Irish National Library. Our walk there took us across a broad sidewalk where American flags with swastikas in the place of stars had been stenciled on the concrete following a march against the war.

It was harder than I would have expected to walk across those faded and disfigured flags every morning. It was harder to see, every day, the sign left hanging in the window across the courtyard from our apartment, an angry denunciation of our country, that we loved, even if we could not disagree with what the sign said. The Irish are generally a friendly people and most we met were kind, but there were moments: the clerk at a corner store who tartly observed, when my wife mentioned how weak the dollar was compared to the Euro, "that's because your president is an idiot." The gentle woman at an Airbnb in the countryside who leaned forward to tell us she couldn't stand what America was doing.

We had come to Dublin, in part, to escape the responsibility of our adult lives, which includes engaging morally and politically with your country. We were in Ireland on an academic fellowship for my wife, but it was also meant to be six-weeks away from all that and everything else. And here we were, in the long shadow of an unpopular and mistaken war, wanting only our own private peace.

Selfish? Yes. Privileged? Of course. But perhaps understandable and something that can be forgiven. I was 46, my wife was 40, and we had been working hard for a long time. We were ready for a break.

Plastic dinosaurs came to our rescue. They were not alone. The principal instigator of our escape was our four-year-old daughter, who was going to preschool in a country where her supposedly English speaking teachers had rural Irish brogues so thick neither my wife or I ever understood half of what they said, and where the kids had the same and were rougher and more physical than American children. She was, more than us, really, on her own in a foreign land for half of every day.

And she managed, almost always without complaint. But she needed time in her own world, and so we bought her a container of plastic dinosaurs. She played with them in the deep, damp grass of the circular green in the back of the Dublin Castle in the afternoons when it wasn't raining. The green is a magical place, the site of the original dubh linn or "black pool" where Vikings anchored their boats as they founded what became the city. It is attended, still, by ghosts, surrounded by the grey stone walls and turrets of the old castle, with narrow stone channels meant to represent sea serpents winding through the grass in a runic pattern.

My wife and I sat on one of the stone benches ringing the green while our daughter knelt in the green and helped her plastic dinosaurs navigate down the channels, through the damp grass, talking to them now and then in her gentle, thoughtful, four-year-old voice, taking us all at least briefly a distance away from the larger, less kind world.

They were soon invited to join the nightly story that my daughter and I wove together before she went to bed. The story had been going on since she was less than two years old and had as its central characters, Rabbit and Bear, who both had sharply defined characters: Rabbit, smart and somewhat cautious, Bear, not so bright, but with an absolutely unshakeable confidence in his capabilities. Bear often led them into less-than-wise adventures. Rabbit worked to get them out. Our daughter, Zaza, was also there, of course, a voice of wisdom and patience, cautioning them both that perhaps they should flee the forest fire, not make the tiger mad, avoid drinking from the unmarked bottle they had found at the abandoned camp sight.

Now they were joined by the dinosaurs, an anonymous, tag-along gang at first, but loyally following Rabbit, Bear and Zaza as they got in and out of trouble. All of it taking me, as I sat on the edge of her bed, rolling onto the carpet with her as they whole gang jumped off a cliff, farther away from the news of the day, which was still there, crouched outside the doorway of the ever more vivid world into which we happily wandered.

Our time in Ireland reached its expiration date. We moved back to Tucson, arriving late on an evening when it was still 107 degrees, the mountains above the city were on fire, the graduate student who had been minding our house, thinking we were landing that morning, had turned off the air conditioning before leaving, and our country was still stuck in a meaningless war. The house would take all night to cool down. The mountains would burn for days. The war would go on for the next dozen years.

We also returned to the mundane realities of daily life: bills to pay, difficult colleagues for my wife to manage, various house breakdowns and repairs. Nothing special. The kind of things everyone deals with. Still, it had a wearying, cumulative effect. I look back now and I realize these were some of the best days of my life—happily married, watching our daughter grow up, yet at the time I was often restless, bored, vaguely dissatisfied.

The dinosaurs came home with us. Their names, I learned, were Littlefoot, Cera, Spike and Petrie, purely coincidentally the names of the characters in the Land Before Time movies, of which we had now watched a couple (eventually all). They, too, had their distinct personalities, Littlefoot, kind and concerned, Cera, impatient and brave, Spike, silent and methodical, Petrie, scattered and hyper, and they weren't really especially brave, smart or strong; they were as ordinary as you and me in many ways, but no matter how much their anarchic prehistoric world threw at them, they kept going, they never stopped trying, and in all their ordinariness they found a way.

Harry Potter was discovered and the whole dinosaur gang went off to Hogwarts. Jeff Bridges voiced a prince in an animated movie our daughter loved, and since we could never remember the name of the actual character, Jeff Bridges turned up at Hogwarts. Spiderman and a completely made-up Superhero named Lizard Girl, who had the power of "poison tongue" arrived.

They had a hundred adventures or more—confronting senselessly ravenous T-Rex (the would-be oligarchs of the dinosaur world), getting trapped in the Room of Requirement in Hogwarts, battling and defeating Voldemort (yes, I know, he's returned), traveling down strange rivers and into haunted forests, dealing with emergencies large and as small as a lost water bottle, I wish I could remember half of them—and in each there was security, escape, comfort, a reassurance that things could make sense even in a world that made none.

The wars went on. Our daughter grew older, left our shared stories behind. Rabbit and Bear, Littlefoot and the gang, Harry Potter and his crew, even Jeff Bridges were left to manage on their own. They have all done fine.

Our daughter went off to college. My wife died. Insane people took control of the U.S. government and started another war, among other horrible things. Life turned a corner and became as much backward looking as forward. As I stare down the wrong end of the telescope, I miss Rabbit and Bear, Jeff Bridges, Harry Potter, and the dinosaur gang these days more than ever.

So when I came upon this small gathering of plastic dinosaurs trapped in a plastic bag at Savers, the secondhand store, I had no choice but to liberate them for the price of $3.49 plus tax. They will be yours if you bid and win them.

The most important thing to know about plastic dinosaurs is they adapt easily. You can set them down almost anywhere and they will find a way to fit in, to become part of the story you are telling yourself about your day, this place, your life. (They have made me believe the entire story we have been told about the non-plastic dinosaurs going extinct is a myth. They would never have sat around happily munching grass and each other while they slowly died off just because some rock fell out of the sky. They would have found a way. My theory is they lit off into space and are now frolicking somewhere on Mars. Elon Musk is in for a big surprise when he gets there!)

I know this is plausible because I have seen plastic dinosaurs in a rocket ship, also on a flying carpet, and in a time machine. (Did I mention they were friends with Calvin and Hobbes? They were! It was Calvin's time machine.)

The second thing to know about plastic dinosaurs is they live in a world where good and virtue can triumph—where danger is faced and, although it can be hard and courage is required, you can make it through. There is, finally, a benevolent order that can be restored. I don't know why you wouldn't want to live in this world. I don't know why you wouldn't want to give it a chance. Set your plastic dinosaurs down in a patch of grass or sand, it doesn't matter. Believe in their resourcefulness and your own. Imagine the story you are telling yourself as one where the odds are overcome, the seemingly insurmountable obstacles, the ravenous enemy, are defeated because you have pluck, you are braver than you know, cleverer, and you are part of a brother- and sisterhood that is stronger than you thought. Let the possibility lead you. Let a better world come to life. Plastic dinosaurs, who have seen and survived it all, will be right there by your side. All you have to do is believe in them.

The New
Joys of Jell-O®
BRAND
Gelatin Dessert
recipe book

The New Joys of Jello by Alexi L

I remember being pressed and primmed. Thin white thread being sewn between my spine and my cover. I felt the life begin to creep within my pages. My back and front were pressed together as one when I was fully awakened. It was the year 1979 when I was finally released from the cold dark room of the factory and put into a cardboard box. All of the others looked exactly like me. We all had the same recipes within our arsenal. The same vibrant images of red domed jello on a platter, green geometric gelatin swirled with a delightful looking cream and a yellow flute, filled with fruits and foam.

None of us actually knew where we were off to. We had only heard rumours of what would happen next to us. We knew that the ultimate goal was to be bought by a human and used to make recipes, but that was about it. Occasionally we'd hear other whispers about humans. Supposedly their fingers are filled with ridges and lines that you can feel on each one of your pages. They even say that no human has the same ones. But that's what is supposed to make them unique.

What makes us unique is our publishing flaws. Some of us have small rips in our pages. Some of us have backward pages. Some of us even have misprints and the wrong sentences. But some of us really are perfect. I was a perfect one. Other people always said that it pays off to be perfect. If you were a flawed copy than straight to trash you went, never to be seen again. With myself being as perfect as I was, I knew that I would finally get to be held and used by a human, maybe even before anyone else. I knew that one day my recipes would be used, that families would use me to create food and fun memories. I had high hopes for myself so all I could do while being in the cardboard box was imagine what my new life would be like soon.

The cardboard flap was flipped open and a blinding white light blurred all of our visions. We were carefully placed onto a metal shelf in neat rows standing up. For some reason the sweaty clerk who smelled of body odor put me in the very back where no one could even see my perfect pristine cover. I watched all of my friends be taken from me, one by one. Apparently everyone loved jello salads. Even though my first two days were agonizing and filled with wanting and yearning, it only took three full days for a man with dark hair and pale skin to pick me up and take me home.

I sat in a plastic bag with some flimsy bright bowls and spoons on the front seat of his car. They were probably all for me, to hold all of my recipes. I felt the engine of the car vibrate along with my excitement. When he opened the door I saw dark brown carpet and red striped wallpaper. It looked perfect. I felt like I was home.

He grabbed me from the bag and set me on a mahogany wood table. Nothing could contain my excitement. The moment I had created in my head of being opened and used for my first recipe was finally going to come to life. But then he slipped on black rubber gloves. Gloves that I couldn't even feel his fingerprints through. I saw him grab a thin white envelope that smelled of rust and paper. He slipped the envelope within my pages gently closing me shut once more, not even bothering to look at my new slip of paper, filled with new peach creme recipes. He then placed me on a shelf overlooking the kitchen where I watched people come in and out, eating around the table. A table that was not once filled with any jello. My perfect appearance was really all I was. I'm not sure how much time had passed before I finally accepted the fact that I would probably never be used for cooking. So I closed my eyes and let the dust gather on me, hoping it would come to an end.

I'm not sure when I was finally picked up again but I do know that there was a loud bang. I could hear the black door from the living room being pushed open. When I opened my eyes for the first time in what felt like centuries my vision was blurred. The fluorescent lights from the kitchen were blinding but I saw the man from before sprawled on the floor with a man in a dark blue suit on top of him. I noticed that the man who bought me now had hair that was littered with grey strands and his skin was much more wrinkled than before. How many years had I been asleep? His hands were being tied behind his back and a gun was pointed to his head.

Before I knew it, the house was being scoured and the man was dragged from the kitchen through the front door. The men in blue suits were frantically looking around the house before they finally stumbled upon me. Once again I was grabbed by gloved men. But these ones were much more aggressive than the man who bought me. They rapidly flipped through my pages barely stopping to look at my recipes. I felt some of my pages tear at the corners and edges until finally the envelope sandwiched inside of me fell to the floor at their feet. They dropped me to the floor alongside the envelope and I really got to stare at the paper that had lived inside of me for who knows how long. It was thicker than I thought. I saw green papers coming out of the top and heard the mysterious men mumble about finding something dirty.

They took the envelope from me and threw me in another cardboard box. I had always envied the envelope stored within me. It always felt like it had more of a purpose than me. Just a plain white paper with other paper inside of it was worth more than me, a book filled with recipes and information. Even though I had always hated the envelope, I felt emptier than ever without it. I never did speak to it, but it reminded me that I was at least being used for something. It felt like the day I was bought all over again. I was back to being purposeless. So once again I closed my eyes and let more dust collect.

When I finally awoke again I was sitting in a large room filled with random objects. They were all whispering to each other, I think about me. I heard them talking about my colors and the small rips that were in my corners. I didn't want them to know I could hear them though so I kept myself shut, ignoring their voices. But I couldn't help but hear their stories, stories about all of the people who had used them and how excited they were to be used once again. All of the experiences they have had since they left their factories. Some objects were even made within human homes. So I filled myself with their stories, imagining that I was one of them. It made me remember how hopeful I had felt back in the cold dark factory. I still have hope that one day I really will be used by a human. Maybe one day I'll be used for my very own purpose.

commo
sens

The Common Sense Vase by Isabel Lage

Warning: This vase might shatter everything you thought was true and right in this world. If you're content going through life as you have been, then this vase is not suitable for you.

Have you ever put your shoes on the wrong feet? Do you watch loud videos with no headphones on in public? Have you used "reply all" when emailing? Do you block doorways? Stop in the middle of the sidewalk while someone's walking behind you? Have you ever driven the wrong way down a one-way street? Gotten out of your car without putting it in park? Do you repost clickbait headlines on your Instagram stories? Have you used a metal fork to get a bagel out of the toaster? Tested if a pan is hot by touching it? Tested if that pan is still hot by touching it again? Have you pulled a "push" door handle so hard that you broke the handle and fell down? Do you let your uncle on your dad's side drive the boat when it was your turn to tube? Have you ever tried to have a Disney princess moment and feed a wild animal by hand with the confidence that it will recognize your good intentions? Have you ever been mauled by said wild animal? Are you the reason warning labels exist?

I could go on, but let me ask you this: do you consistently feel like the kind of everyday understanding that seems obvious to others evades you: like how magnets work or why deodorant matters? If you answered yes, have I got the vase for you. If you answered no, think of that friend or family member who would have answered yes. Have I got the vase for them!

The Common Sense Vase holds all the answers. A beautiful piece of craftsmanship, the vase features mid-20th-century-inspired shades of brown, 3D texture, and a comfortable weightiness. The cool, smooth feel of the dark brown areas nicely contrasts the coarse texture of the lighter brown and the deep engraving of the words "common sense." It would look stylish on your desk holding pencils or by your bedside holding flowers, but really, the contents you keep in it are of little importance.

The true value of this piece comes from what you can extract from it.

Once a day, simply hold the vase up to your ear, and it will reveal one piece of common sense. Its ergonomic shape fits comfortably in the palm of your hand, making it easy to use. During your first use, you might experience a slight tingling and popping sensation in the ear pressed against the vase's opening. It's vaguely similar to that childhood candy, Pop Rocks. And not to worry. Any sign of infection is pure logic in motion.

One of the first things the vase told me was, "Don't wear cutoff jean shorts to your cousin's wedding." Astounding, I know. But that is just a small snippet of the potential of this vase.

Also, as you know, or you will once you buy this vase, a person can't be book-smart and street-smart. For every piece of common sense, you must give up a more scholastic piece of information: the Pythagorean theorem, how to write in cursive, literature analysis—the useless stuff, really.

It's worth noting the vase won't share its knowledge with anyone besides you, the owner, as long as you are in possession of it. This means that even if you gain all the common sense in the world, there's still a chance no one around you will be willing to listen. Common sense is far too few and far between in this world, and the vase is a rare find indeed. Despite all the things it has told me, its origin remains a mystery that can't be solved through common sense alone.

Convinced I could outsmart it, I tried to make a replica. I carved the words exactly as they appear on the original. I held it up to my ear, and… nothing.

The next day, I picked up the real vase.

"You fool," it whispered. "Have you learned nothing? I am the one and only Common Sense Vase."

A Vaguely Rod of Asclepius Shaped Glass Wine Stop by Jacquelyn Lo Bianco

It was just a gift, something wrapped in thin paper and tucked away in a box. But it was a gift for the achievement of making it through rigorous schooling. Nursing school already gave her late nights, mountains of reports, and haunting visions, but the contents of the box made Mary smile. The top was delicate glass in the shape of a squiggle that weaved around to form a crescent, beautiful blue and green coloring the translucent material. If she looked closer, the movement of the glass resembled the wings of the Rod of Asclepius while the bottom half was the snakes wrapped around the staff. Mary knew what the gift was; a move towards the promise of wine nights after long shifts at the hospital.

Two weeks after Mary's first full shift in the progressive care unit was when she put her gift to use. The cork of her cabernet sauvignon ripped in two at the force of her taking it out of the bottle. Mary was glad the glass neck hadn't shattered at the thought of how her supervisor treated her the entire shift.

"Are you sure you know how much to administer? The doctor's orders say here—"

"Don't let the flow go too fast, Mary, they taught you that in school right?"

"Mr. Smith can be out of his senses sometimes, that doesn't mean he knew what he did to you. Just forget about it and continue your work."

The grating voice of the older woman rang in Mary's ears even after her third glass was consumed. Mary had trained for four years to become a nurse, yet the elder nurse hovered around her like a pesky fly rather than attending to her own patients. When the warmth and floating feeling had dulled the sounds of voices, machines beeping, and made Mary's eyes hang low, she placed the winestop in its first bottle.

It didn't matter what type of bottle of wine Mary chose—rosé, sauvignon blanc, merlot—it was always topped with the blue-green glass stopper. Visiting coworkers always said it was beautiful and asked where she got it, but the response was the same:

"It was a gift."

She never spoke the gifter's name outloud, yet her heart pounded the rhythm of their name's syllables. The one who was beside her during those long years of schooling.

Her partners always knew that if the winestop was in the sink, leave it for Mary to clean. The first time one of Mary's ex-boyfriends picked it up to clean, the suds on his hands from the other dishes made his hands too slick and the smooth glass escaped from his grasp. The clatter it made against the bottom of the sink had Mary jolting from the couch and appearing in seconds to check the delicate thing. That was their first fight in the relationship and Mary made it a rule from that moment on. No one touched it except her.

That rule broke when Mary's former classmate came to her apartment for their long overdue wine night. When Mary pulled out her bottle of pinot noir with the wine stop in her other hand, her classmate laughed, the loud and obnoxious one she remembered from the late nights in the library, at the sight of it.

"You kept it. After how many years now?"

"Enough for hundreds of wine nights."

Mary gave it to her classmate to hold, to admire how the blue-green glass shined in the dim room. As the two classmates caught up, the wine stop sat on the coffee table sparkling from the warm lights and that night was the first night where its service wasn't needed. The wine stop sat there listening to stories it had heard over the years from different bottles of wine. Hysterical laughter and silent tears came paired with the words that felt like the same situation over and over.

"You should take it with you."

"It was a gift for you though, I can't take it."

"Well I'm giving it back to you. You'll need it more than me."

"It's official then?"

"Yup, my two weeks are approved. I'll be gone before they know it."

That was the last time Mary saw the wine stop. She gave it back to the person who gifted it to her in the first place with the hope it would mean the same as it did for her. Mary was leaving the field her classmate still had so much passion for, so she didn't know how many more wine nights the glass wine stop had left in its life. She didn't know of the wine stop's fate after that night, but herself and the gifter wished that the next person to use it would care for the delicate piece just as they had.

The Good, The Bad, The Ugly: A Hot Pepper Eating Contest (Hot Pepper Salsa Dish) by Sean Lovelace

I have run far, very far, Chicago, Boston, other marathons, ultramarathons. Fished large fish from the deep sea. Hunted big game down, harvested said game with a bow and arrow and string, cooked and ate its flesh in the backcountry over a low fire, under high Pleiades, under the eye of Orion (another hunter). I have conquered the world of professional disc golf—Ok, factually, I was for several years an amateur champion of a motley, bedraggled group of disc golf obsessed friends (maybe eight or so devotees of the art and science of flying plastique), but still. I once rolled 11 consecutive games of bowling. Attempted to drink, in one evening at a Michigan dive bar, every single variety of beer on tap. (I made it through 9.5.) Ate nachos 141 days in a row. And so? I am a man of quests. For a while I'd been thinking of entering a hot pepper eating contest. I'd seen *Hot Ones* on YouTube. Watched *Man Versus Food* (a show that had to change its host due to health issues—go figure). Sat on my couch riveted as Joey Chestnut vanquished his foes on the 4th of July. I felt I could do it. I could not only survive the heat, but I could also win. And then, the Fire Up DWNTWN Festival arrived in Muncie.

THE GOOD: The Fire Up DWNTWN Festival was pretty boss: the theme was fire/flame/conflagration. Good energy, good crowds, decent food (I had some nachos), live music, a couple hot air balloons shooting out tongues of flames, a parade of jeeps and their owners (I wasn't sure how this related to fire but whatever), a couple women twirling flaming batons, and a group of hipster dudes welding iron and pouring molten liquid in an attempt to create a statue of Bob Ross. (I was actually dressed as Bob Ross that day—giant afro, blue jeans, brown shoes, aviator glasses, button down open-necked with peace necklace twinkling, paintbrush in pocket—but that is irrelevant here. That's a whole different essay.)

THE BAD: The sun was blasting. The temp was approaching mid-90's and rising as the contest time neared. Dressing as Bob Ross—jeans, the heat-trapping afro (a wig), etc.—was poor judgement. There would be additional poor judgement forthcoming.

THE GOOD: I wasn't daunted. I felt somewhat confident. I have eaten hot sauces of various Scoville Heat Units (a metric invented by a pharmacologist Wilbur Lincoln Scoville in 1912 to measure the pungency of peppers and chilies, generally related to their capsaicin content, the fieriest of compounds) for over thirty years. At this point in my life, hot sauce was to me like ketchup to others, or perhaps since this was all taking place in Indiana, ranch dressing. Or mayonnaise. How different could the raw peppers be than the hot sauce?

THE BAD: Time to sign the legal waiver. O the waiver…

I stood in line at the restaurant (The Clubhouse) that organized the hot pepper eating contest. The restaurant would close a few months later, primarily because its business model involved a row of golf simulators for $35 an hour. Most locals don't have that type of expendable income. Also, the food was bad. Like a lot of Midwesterners, Muncie folks don't mind bad food, but it must be in large servings and affordable. They don't need golf with lunch.

A guy in front of me said, "You enter these often?"

"First time," I said. He smirked.

Wait, there's going to be professionals here? My stomach rumbled. And then I saw him, a stout man with a beard wearing a furry hat in the shape of a red pepper. He seemed relaxed as a Jell-O shot. I'd been warned about him from my work colleague, the Mayor of Muncie (unofficial title and a long story—he knows everyone in the entire town). Yep, it was Defending Champ. The Mayor of Muncie said D Champ had won the contest three years in a row and then told me a story (which I prayed was apocryphal) wherein he snorted a line of crushed jalapeño seeds on a bet.

THE GOOD (I guess…): We had enough time to grab one beer (my partner ordered a margarita served in a plastic bucket) and go to the car for my Unscientific Preparation:

- Drank a half gallon of vanilla toasted coconut soy milk. I heard somehow milk cuts the bite of hot peppers. This was an error. Only dairy milk contains the protein that helps neutralize capsaicin.
- Drank a two liter of diet ginger ale.
- Drank the beer.
- Ate a gummy multivitamin.
- Ate two Advil.
- Ate 4 Pepto Bismol 5-Symptom Stomach Relief, Nausea Relief, Heartburn Relief, Indigestion Relief, and Diarrhea Relief caplets.

THE BAD: The owner of the restaurant looked like an overly happy Barney Fife, though I suppose Barney was mostly overly happy.

He said, "Hey everyone! Welcome! I want y'all to know we had six people make it to the eighth round last year so we are making this year extra hot. Had to do a lot of searching but we found the hottest peppers in the world!"

My forehead furrowed; stomach gurgled. I glanced around to catch a sympathetic eye. The contestants were chatting, drinking beer. One woman high-fived the other woman in line.

The owner brought over a cardboard box and handed us each what appeared to be a blue plastic sock. It had increments printed on the side in metrical units. What the?

A vomit bag.

THE BAD: Shall we quote from the waiver?

"…must be 18 years or older."

"…shall not be held responsible or liable for any action in which I elect to consume any food that may…"

"I hereby forever release and hold harmless The Heat is On Pepper Eating Contest."

"…have been known to cause undesired effects such as overall discomfort, abdominal or gastro-intestinal discomfort, flush, dizziness, extreme burning sensation, tearing, numbing, tingling and post digestive discomfort on a temporary and/or possible permanent basis."

"I acknowledge that there could be a risk of personal injury, illness and possible loss of life…"

Loss of life?

THE BAD: We climbed up onto a rickety stage above a teeming (and probably inebriated) crowd. My partner, well into the tequila by now, yelled out, "Go Bob Ross!" A kid wearing a red apron appeared and played "taps" on a tinny horn, then returned to the shade of the restaurant. The sun was ablaze; sweat trickled down from the corners of my afro. Barney Fife leapt onto the stage with a microphone, waving his arms, ready to MC, ready to read The Rules from a sheet of paper. My adrenaline was kicking up. I hardly remember all the rules, but the Mayor of Muncie gave me a copy a few weeks later, so I quote:

The Heat is On Hot Pepper Eating Contest Rules

All contestants agree to take part in the contest under the following rules:

1. Participants must be 18 years of age or older.
2. The contest will consist of a series of rounds with participants able to withdraw at any stage, either during the round or before the next round begins.
3. The peppers will begin at milder heat and will increase based on the Scoville scale as rounds progress. Peppers will be announced before each round with their corresponding Scoville Heat Units (SHUs).
4. Each contestant will receive the pepper for that round at the beginning of that round.
5. Contestants will be required to eat the entire pepper- flesh, seeds and membrane (not stem).
6. Contestants will be allowed to finish any pepper remaining in their mouths when time is called after 1 minute. The rule does not apply to tie breaker situation defined in Rule 8.
7. The winner will be determined by being the last remaining contestant willing to continue the contest.
8. In the event of a tie, remaining contestants will be given a food item from The Clubhouse to eat, and the first one to finish the item in the determination of the judge will be declared the winner.
9. Contestants may not coat the inside of their mouths with any kind of protective coating and will be disqualified if caught doing so, in sole determination of the judge.
10. Each contestant will be given a glass of milk to consume when desired, but drinking any liquid, including the milk provided, will result in being disqualified.
11. Any contestant that vomits either during the round or within the one minute period after the round has completed will be disqualified.

12. Each contestant recognizes that excess consumption of peppers can lead to or contribute to health issues.
13. The judge's decision is final.

I remember thinking it was pretty twisted you could be offered milk during the contest, but if you accept the milk, you instantly lose…

THE GOOD: There was zero chance I would drink the milk. I don't drink milk, not cow milk. Only baby cows should drink cow milk.

THE GOOD (potentially): First place was a trophy, $100 restaurant credit, and the title of Badass. Second was $50 credit. Third was $30 credit.

THE BAD: We took our seats, and introduced ourselves and I said into the microphone, playing to the crowd, "My name is Bob."

Some folks laughed, shouted. Back in the day, Bob Ross filmed his painting show in Muncie, about a mile from where we were sitting.

I surveyed my competition, eight men, two women. The man on my left I assumed was from Afghanistan because he looked like he was from Afghanistan, and I knew for a fact many Afghan families had settled in Muncie after the 2021 fall of Kabul. D Champ (his name was Casey) sat on my right. I noticed one man appeared to be dressed as a banana. The others seemed goofy, happy, I guess ready, smiling. My heart clanged. It was go-time. The first raw pepper arrived on a small white paper plate, placed on the table by a young lady wearing rubber gloves.

"Rocotillo!" Barney Fife shouted to the crowd.

The pepper (2,000 Scoville) was a cherry red, warped and squished like some caterpillar in pain.

Remembering the rule about eating it all—" flesh, seeds and membrane"—I popped the entire thing in my mouth, crunched twice, swallowed.

It was hot. Hotter than I thought the very first pepper had a right to be. Dread appeared, a smidgen of doubt. I guess I was caught unawares for a moment. Then the heat slightly dissipated...Ok, I thought. OK.

THE GOOD: Peppers two (jalapeño, 8,000 Scoville) and three (Black Cobra, 40,000) I considered less spicy than pepper one. I ate them both, smiled, pounded my fist on the table to charge up the crowd. "Bob Ross!" my partner shouted from off somewhere.

The two women and Banana Man stood, waved goodbye, and stepped off the stage.

Now we were seven.

THE BAD: Barney Fife spun on his heels, threw up his hands, and shouted "Roxa!"

First thing, this was a large pepper. A deep blood red. Shimmering. 80,000 Scoville. It wasn't going to be one bite and swallow. I took a bite, second bite, chewed a bit, swallowed twice, a slight gagging. My mouth went from the steady burning of the previous peppers to a more urgent sensation very difficult to describe: a blistering curtain falling from the uvula to the lips, and my head involuntarily lowered. The tips of my fingers tingled. The very edges of my vision quivered, and filled with what appeared to be shimmering, cracked glass...

Two contestants stood, one wobbled, let out an enormous belch, then they both walked off the stage.

Five remained. I studied each: D Champ looked like he was at a picnic on a green lawn, perhaps in New England. Not a worry. Afghanistan stared ahead stoically. The three others I could see the effects (my vision now surrounded in a black, hazy circle): sweat, flushed face, agony.

THE GOOD: I don't remember pepper five.

THE GOOD/BAD: Pepper six was a ghost, at one million Scoville. I was very familiar with the ghost from many a hot sauce. A raw pepper is not a hot sauce (one of many lessons I would learn that day). Hot sauce is cut with vinegar, xanthan gum, salt, lime juice, etc.

I ate the ghost and now my mouth roared; seemed to have its own pulse or beat. My fingers were numb, and the feeling (or loss of) climbed up into my wrists. My left foot glowed, as if asleep. My vision collapsed further: now I was squinting through a tunnel, way off an echo, "Bob Ross…Bob Ross." Then someone screamed!

A contestant had accidently touched their own eye. They stumbled off the stage and was absorbed by the crowd. A second contestant calmly stood up and walked away.

My arms were shaking, my hands failing. My mouth had a metallic taste I recalled from childhood fevers. My temples throbbed. I could only see about 30% of my normal field of vision. But I made top three. Afghanistan, D Champ, me.

THE BAD: At 1.4 million Scoville, the "Trinidad Scorpion 'Butch T'" was the hottest pepper in the world in 2011. (This was before the Wabash Valley Pepper Fest & Hot Sauce Expo Controversy, before the laboratory and gene-splicing arms race, etc.)

From what I could see (and, at this point, I could not see much), it resembled the contorted heart of a small animal, torn from its chest, dyed emerald green, and dried in the relentless desert sun.

I took a deep breath, placed it in my mouth, chewed—gagged, hacked, almost had a reversal (vomit bag in hand), gagged, gagged, fought it back, swallowed. And the interplanetary began.

The arms were limp, gone. Heart tripping, then clacking, a strange cadence. All went black. I was slowly levitating, off the chair, above the crowd…floating, floating…I had a vision of a long white dining table in a dimly lit room and I sat alone at one end and way off at the other end a dark figure, hunched…in the center of the table, on an impeccably clean white tablecloth, sat a white bowl full of some white, swirling cloud-like material, and the dark figure seemed to gesture to the bowl, eat, eat… I snapped back to a voice booming over the microphone, "Pepper number eight, folks! Unknown to nature! Built by science! The Reaper!"

THE UGLY: Through a grainy, tiny pinhole, I could see pepper eight, all 2.2 million Scoville, slim, a devil's pinky, a dagger, though it seemed to be in black and white. I stared at it, time slipping away… my hands wouldn't move. My brain sent a message: pick up the pepper. Pick. Up. The Pepper. The hands refused. Something clattered. A hawk called out, or perhaps a crying child…My chair fell back, I slipped, stumbled, caught myself. I was off the stage, how? Down by a garbage can and a graffitied brick wall; I took a deep breath of wet, rank garbage—someone handed me an envelope. I moaned. Something was on my face. Mucus. Tears. I staggered away, behind the stage, down an alley…the voices of the crowd drifting. My partner arrived—poof!—grabbed my shoulder, and said, "Are you okay?"

"I gnard the kore," I slurred, hacking, snorting.

"What?"

I fell over, wiped snot off my face with my shirt, righted myself, coughed out, "I can't see the core. The car. I need the car."

"You need to vomit!" she said. "That's the only way. Go ahead and vomit."

She took the envelope from my clenched hand and grabbed the other hand and we headed to the car.

"You really need to vomit," she said the entire way.

The last thing I remember from the event was kneeling on a curb by the back tires of the car, guzzling down Pepto and soy milk, spitting, guzzling, spitting…

Several people walked by on their way to the festival and either circled far around me, or peered close and said, "Hey, are you OK? Are you OK… I mean are you OK?"

THE GOOD: A few days later I learned the results from the Mayor of Muncie: D Champ won. Well, congratulations.

THE BAD: Afghanistan got second but was admitted to the hospital right after the event.

THE GOOD: That's it for me. Never, ever again. Officially retired. But I did it. A respectful third place. A few weeks later my partner and I spent the $30 prize on lunch: she had a quesadilla though the kitchen had neither sour cream on hand nor salsa (both were listed as part of the order).

"I can run across the street and try to get you some sour cream," the waitress kept saying.

We answered that wouldn't be necessary.

I looked out the window, to the street. The stage was gone. A light rain dappled down. A dog trotted by, and pigeons picked at something. I studied the menu. I ordered the nachos.

24
Crayola®
MADE WITH SOLAR POWER*
Preferred by Teachers!
CRAYONS
24
Nontoxic

Crayolas, Gently Used by Juan Martinez

These Crayolas arrived from my cousin J— D—, as did these two photographs, as did a note (not included in the sale) shortly before he moved away from his house in Toronto, Ontario, and from his wife and his two young daughters. J— D— had a long and, as far as I could tell, happy career in financing. He did some consulting work for McKinsey in Bogota beforehand. He left Colombia when we all did, in the early aughts, just as kidnappings hit their peak, and he pursued a life of prosperity and stability in prosperous, stable Canada—a life that to my eyes felt thoroughly reasonable, though to be fair neither one of us was that great at keeping in touch, and so what I saw or knew of him was mostly via Facebook or the irregular update from my mother, who had an uncanny ability to keep in touch with everyone in our family. He was fine, my mom told me. He'd gained some weight, she said, and seemed a little sad; he'd taken up smoking again, but his wife was lovely, his children too: the children were learning Spanish, the wife not so much, which was a shame. But other than that? Fine, just fine. And fine—just fine—is how I thought of my cousin, if I thought of him at all, until exactly twenty years ago: he visited me and my soon-to-be wife in Las Vegas, his visit practically unannounced—he missed me, he wrote. We had just announced our wedding on Facebook the week before. I assumed that had prompted the email and subsequent visit. J— D— arrived and insisted that I take him to a strip club; I had just picked him up, we were in my car, had not even made it out of the airport. I assumed that he was just going a little feral, that he was doing what he supposed people did when they came to our city. I said no. I said no like ten times, relented after the eleventh time. The strip club was as depressing: as desultory and dispiring as you can imagine. Just, like, deeply, deeply unarousing. I felt sad in there. And J— D— looked sad, and manic, and he held a wad of bills high, spent a considerable chunk on lap dances. He said, You'll do this too, one day. When you have children. I said no. You artists, he said, between cigarettes: he'd gone back to Camels, the same brand we both smoked in Bogota. *You artists think you're so pure,* he said. *I'm taking art classes,* he said. *It's not that hard, what you do.* I told him I didn't draw, that I wrote, that it was a whole different thing. J— D— shook his head: *You make things, you pretend you're so special. You're just children. I can do it too, you know. Children can do what you do, they do it all the time, they don't think they're special. I can do that and I can make money. Guess which one's harder? And guess which one makes you sad?* Then he repeated himself: *You'll do this too, you'll come to strip clubs, it all changes when you have children.* I said no, and I was right, and I didn't understand why he was telling me this, why he was here at all. I said, *I guess you can't do this in Toronto.* He said, *I go to strip clubs all the time in Toronto. That's all I do, when I am not at home.* Another cigarette. *I don't tell my wife,* he said. I told him that I told my wife everything. *She's not your wife,* he said, *not yet.* I coughed. *No, no you don't.* He'd gone through most of his pack of Camels. *And no you won't,* he added. *You'll see. She's not your wife yet, at any rate, and my wife would leave me if she ever found out. I've been coming to these places for years. She's never found out. Listen,* he said, *we need to go to another strip club, I looked it up, there's one just across the street, right by that drugstore, right next to that weird custard shack.* We walked under the heat and glow of the Stratosphere. He bought me a custard, refused one himself because he was trying to lose weight. *One day,* he said, *I'll get good enough to draw the strippers. I'll draw them nude. They're art,* he said. *OK,* I said. He said, *I read Bukowski, you know. I read all sorts of people. You're not special.* He flew home the next day, and I heard of his disappearance from my mother decades later—he's fine, she clarified. Safe. The family, my mother told me, is distraught of course, the wife livid. I imagined my cousin out there, drawing, but my mother said that he'd actually flown to Orlando, to interview for an apprenticeship not far from my old university: an artist known for large-scale collages prominently featured in the lobbies of some of the world's finest Marriotts. J— D— had been taken under the famous hotel artist's wing. I've since read about the artist, about the circumstances around his disappearance. I cannot speak too much about my cousin's note or about the particular instructions and disclosures contained in the note. I can only insist that you please strongly consider not opening the box of Crayolas, that my cousin is alive and well, that his sadness has finally lifted, that he is not responsible for the artist's disappearance, that he has mailed other gently-used art supplies to other family members—all those supplies now presumably also listed on eBay, as per his instructions—and that we are all, my mother included, under strict instructions to share only what little we're allowed, to let you know that he is fine now. He is free. He is determined to keep doing whatever it is he thinks he is doing.

I cannot confirm whether my cousin's drawing is, in fact, wedged into the box; it may very well be; he has asked that you not share any of this information with his wife. They are somehow still married. She is not allowed to bid on this item.

Gardening and Other Verbs (Garden Angel) by Andrew Maynard

He aspired to be the type of father who gardened with his sons. Imagined their hands submerged in soil while he YouTubed how to build a planter with treated wood and a circle saw. Googled the pros and cons of wood varieties and envisioned pressing the rotating blade into the cedar and sliding it with the exact pressure and cadence that his mother had used to iron his khakis on Sunday mornings. After the service she always made him change clothes before they gardened, and there was a time he knew his way around the dirt, as if his palms and fingers could see. And he tried to reremember that feeling of knowing, truly knowing—muscle memory, instinct, experience-divided-by-theory—as he uploaded a photo of his drooping, overgrown lawn for ChatGPT to discern which corner might best welcome the sun. He briefly considered filling the wooden frame before him with sand and simply letting his boys play with buckets and shovels, but he couldn't shed the possibility that just maybe they could build something to last, to sustain, to regenerate. And if he and his boys could, then maybe she already did. He pictured the topsoil above her wooden frame—rich, balanced, tunneled with worms—then shut his computer, plucked his phone from his pocket, and called the landline still mounted in the vine-covered house he couldn't bring himself to sell, not yet, no, not quite yet, to deliver the message of his intentions in hopes that maybe words are more like seeds than he'd ever let himself believe.

Coke ORIGINAL TASTE
Nutrition Facts

Can/Glove Coozie by Porter Norton McDonald

June 27, 1990

MEMO: Thank you for the years of hard work!

ATTN: EMPLOYEES

This week we would like to our recognize and celebrate Ameri(Can) Co. family. Your loyalty and dedication has allowed us to continue to produce quality and innovative canned goods on a global level. To show our appreciation, you will find a Special Gift at your workspace. Make sure to bring your Special Gift to the annual company picnic (details below). There will be games! Thank you and keep up the YES WE CAN! spirit!

What: Ameri(Can) Co. Fourth of July Picnic
When: Wednesday, July 4th 11 AM-2 PM
Where: Itchy Hole Lake Recreation Center (Ramadas 4-7)

June 28, 1990

MEMO: Special Gift: Explanation

ATTN: EMPLOYEES

In the past twenty-four hours, we have received several questions from employees unclear as to the function of their Special Gift. The Can/Glove Coozie is an insulation sleeve for canned beverages as well as a fingerless glove. The glove has been sewn to the can in order to attach the user to their drink. After consulting with the designer, we have confirmed that the glove and Coozie are meant to stay together as a single unit.

June 28, 1990

MEMO: Thank you Carl Sturgis!

ATTN: EMPLOYEES

We would like to extend a very special thank you to Carl Sturgis for his design of the Can/Glove Coozie and for his twenty-three years of creativity and innovation as Art Director and Head of Product Design at the Ameri(Can) Co. Make sure to show your appreciation by wearing your Can/Glove Coozie to the company picnic next Wednesday. There will be games!

What: Ameri(Can) Co. Fourth of July Picnic

When: Wednesday, July 4th 11 AM-2 PM

Where: Itchy Hole Lake Recreation Center (Ramadas 4-7)

June 29, 1990

MEMO: Can/Glove Coozie: Protocol

ATTN: EMPLOYEES

Please do not wear your Can/Glove Coozie during working hours. Remember, we need two hands to be a productive member of the Ameri(Can) family. Thank you and see you at the picnic.

July 2, 1990

MEMO: Beverages at workstations

ATTN: EMPLOYEES

Computers are delicate and expensive pieces of equipment. They are also not waterproof. Starting today, all drinks must be kept in the break rooms only. ABSOLUTELY NO BEVERAGES AT WORKSTATIONS.

REMINDER: Please do not wear your Can/Glove Coozie during working hours. Save it for the company picnic this Wednesday.

July 3, 1990

MEMO: Can/Glove Coozie Trade

ATTN: EMPLOYEES

In light of recent concerns regarding the Can/Glove Coozie, administration is now offering alternative gifts in the break room for any employee wishing to trade their Coozie for a more "appreciative" item. Choices include:

- A Can-a-Day Desk Calendar
- Ameri(Can) Co. Frisbee
- 6-Pack of Roller ball pens

July 3, 1990

MEMO: Can/Glove Coozie Trade: Clarification

ATTN: EMPLOYEES

The gift offerings in the break room are meant to replace the Can/Glove Coozie. In order to receive a calendar, or frisbee, YOU MUST FIRST TRADE IN YOUR CAN/GLOVE Coozie. Items are limited to one per employee. Roller-ball pens are no longer an option but are available in the supply closet (one per employee).

July 5, 1990

MEMO: "Yes we can!"

ATTN: EMPLOYEES

Thank you to those of you who attended the Ameri(Can) Co. Fourth of July Picnic yesterday and for showing the YES WE CAN spirit, especially in retrieving the skuttled paddle boats. Just a reminder, please take your Can/Glove Coozies home. All work must be done with two hands!

July 5, 1990

MEMO: Two Hands correction

ATTN: EMPLOYEES

It was recently brought to our attention that it was insensitive to suggest that all employees are physically able to work with two hands. To our disabled employees, we sincerely apologize.

July 6, 1990

MEMO: Can/Glove Coozie Forbidden

ATTN: EMPLOYEES

Any employee wearing the can/glove Coozie during working hours will receive a disciplinary write-up. Please direct any questions to H.R.

Hamburglar Responds to McDonald's CEO Chris Kempczinski's Viral Burger-"Eating" Video (Vintage Hamburglar Figurine) by Ted McLoof

H **Burglar, Ham - (hamburglar)** <hamburglar@gmail.com> Mar 6, 2026 2:16 PM (1 min ago)
to McDonald's HQ

Dear McDonald's Marketing Team, or to Whom it May Concern,

I'm going to try my absolute best not to lose my temper in this email response. Despite your company's efforts in the past to alter my public persona, I consider myself a pretty rational, even-tempered guy. I've stolen a few of your burgers in the past, sure, whatever, but you paid me and the rest of your staff minimum wage without benefits. How was I supposed to feed my wife and kids? That's a You problem.

That said, after watching the viral "ad" where your current CEO Chris Kempczinski (Chris K, as he so phonily attempts colloquially to be called) takes a reluctant, mouse-sized bite of your new Big Arch burger only after a full minute of staring at it like it's rancid…

My only response is: What the fuck?

I know, I know: I literally *just* said I'd keep my cool but whatever, the moment demands the tone. I'm not going to pussyfoot around this.

I'll give you this: you want a bland, middle-aged white guy with dead eyes to play corporate robot to the shareholders and exploit the proletariat behind a velvet curtain, sure. Chris K's your guy. But you want someone who's camera ready? Someone with charisma? Someone with blood in his veins and cholesterol in his heart from years—decades—of eating your "product" and who won't creep people out? And you bring in *this fucking guy?*

Not only is he clearly not the man for the job, but you've got me RIGHT. HERE. Granted, I'm a *former* employee. You haven't hired me since that cameo you threw me in '23, and it was forever before that. I'll pretend I don't know why. Surely it can't be my criminal record. Your history with prison labor in Alabama would suggest you have no qualms about indentured servitude. Maybe it was my big mouth? Maybe I had one too many vodka sodas one too many times and said one too many things about how you treat your employees and how the McSausage gets made?

But I'm past that now. You could have brought me back in. People fucking love nostalgia these days. Jimmy Fallon's built a whole career off of it. Do you have any clue what I would have done to that burger? I would have *slaughtered* it. I would have *housed* it. I would have *fellated* it. You wouldn't have been able to hit "record" on whatever un-miced iPhone you filmed on before it hit the recesses of my throat. You would have had to hand me another one. And another. And another. I wouldn't have called that shit "product"; I would have sold it. I would have made just as much love to the camera as I would to that burger. Chris K asks, "How do I attack this thing?" How? You think I wouldn't have known how to attack a burger? Attacking burgers is how I got locked up. HamAttacker just doesn't sound as good.

McDonald's, you beautiful awful golden godless greasetrap of a capitalist monster you: we could have had something beautiful. We could have sold pink slime AND saved the world. What's that Thomas Friedman quote, about no two countries with a McDonald's ever having gone to war? The wounds we could have healed. I mean, it was bullshit, he was wrong, Russia's got plenty of McDonald's and what's left of Ukraine has them too, but we could have continued to sell that lie together! What do you have now instead? Some ragebait? A bunch of uncreative freelance digital losers writing op-ed pieces about how you actually *"meant"* to make an ad that terrible for clicks? Please.

I would have done anything you asked. I'll strip naked and bathe in special sauce. I'll change my kids' names to Ronald and Grimace. I'll canvas for Mayor McCheese. I'll eat that Big Mac that guy left out for a year that never grew mold. I'll drink shamrock shakes straight from the machine and wash them down with Rumpelminz until I spew, I'll eat the McRib and I'll never once ask which animal's rib it comes from, though I have my suspicions. I'll sing lullabies to my kids that go, "Two all-beef patties special sauce lettuce cheese pickles onions all on a sesame seed bun." I'll burn my forearm to the nerves in fry oil if you ask. I'll testify in court that no, Your Honor, I never got a tour of the factories and couldn't tell you what the conditions are. I'll ride on top of the golden arches like they're magical corporate golden camel humps and post pictures humping those humps all over Instagram if you ask. I'll serve burgers in the drive-thru just like your man Trump did. I'll let you super size me. You don't like the prison-striped suit? Throw me in a t-shirt. You think the pork pie hat is too Walter White? I'll wear a trucker hat if it makes me more approachable (just *please* don't make me wear a MAGA hat; I have my dignity).

This is what you've brought me to. I love you, McDonald's, and I hate and fear you, and I can't live without you. I know all of your secrets and I see through your bullshit and still you've brought me to my knees. Don't lock me out anymore. I so badly want to be back in headquarters. We're starving out here, McDonald's. Can't you see? I won't talk shit anymore if you let me in. Ray Kroc can suck a dick. Sorry. That one slipped. I need you. Don't you need me? Are you lovin' it? Have you had your break today?

Sincerely,
The Hamburglar

Letters Found Within a Statuette by Christian Moher and Eliza Moher

Dear Calum—

Father is gone again, this time I fear (or hope) it is for good. He took everything, of course, but I had the foresight this time to hide a few items to keep us going until you return. Mother is worse. She does not leave the house anymore. Honestly, she does not leave her bed. I fear she will be leaving me soon as well. If she dies, then I will not be able to stay here and wait for you to come home.

I was searching yesterday in father's closet, and underneath a loose floorboard I found a small ceramic figurine of a noble child of some sort, well-fed and a bit portly with very sad eyes. Father must have forgotten it was there because I am sure he would have sold it if he remembered. There is a weathered piece of paper hidden inside that I cannot get to for fear of breaking the statue, but I will keep working on it and let you know if it is anything of value.

I think of you often, and I hope that you are safe and warm, though if the news reports are to be believed it seems like you are likely suffering and cold and perhaps injured. It is those thoughts that prevent me from sleeping at night, and also wishing that you could have had a normal childhood, a normal life-but you are not normal, and if the government is to be believed then you have skills that are much needed in these dark times.

I am selling the last of the silverware today, and may have to pawn mother's wedding band soon. That would leave us nothing of value for next month, but that is my burden, not yours. Yours is to survive and come back to me. I am not certain this letter will reach you as I don't know where you are, but I will put my trust in an untrustworthy government to get this to you safely.

If you return and I am gone, look for me at the oak tree where we found the snake with two heads.

Your sister,

A

Dearest A,

I'm surprised your letter found me. They have us moving so often I'm afraid I've become disoriented, I have no idea where I am, even who I am. I fear they do it on purpose, keep us mobile so our guards never fall. The cold is numbing, though it's the least of our concerns. In earnest, most days are quiet, filled with excruciating waiting.

It seems father was always best at leaving rather than staying, so his sudden departure from this Earth is entirely unsurprising. I do apologize that you must bear this on your own, but you always were the clever one out of the two of us, mother always said so.

To hear of mother's condition concerns me, if she departs before my return, feel no reason to stay in that damned house. Wherever you go I will not be far behind, I will see to it that I find you as soon as these knaves give me my leave. Do not feel remorse, your leaving that house has been postponed for far too long, and I worry that someone of your sensitive nature will be eaten alive by the secrets that inhabit those walls.

The figurine you mention disturbs me, it's unlike father to keep something of such a nature and not attempt to sell it, it's possible it meant a great deal to him. Perhaps he left it for us to find on purpose, though, if the parchment hidden inside is some sort of message for the two of us, I'm not sure if it's something I wish to see. As horrible as it sounds, part of me wishes to ignore it, and leave the bastard and his words buried deep into the ground. But I know, my dear sister, that your curiosity is insatiable, so if you wish to read the note, listen to these instructions carefully: Do not break it. If it's even close to what I think it could be, its main purpose is containment. They briefed us on these relics during our training, and if the ceramic shell is broken, you will find yourself in grave danger. I struggle to understand why father would leave you to find such a great potential threat, but I can only assume the words he's stashed inside are of great importance. Grab the forceps from mother's bed chamber, quietly so she doesn't ask questions. If you can obtain the parchment safely, without damaging the figure, do so. If that doesn't work, I fear we must exercise our comfort in ignorance, and you must hide the figure where no one will ever find it again. The risk of it breaking and unleashing whatever horrors may lay inside cause me great worry, and I fear those horrors may have caused our father's demise. Our world as we know it can not handle it. Bury it, hide it deep in the cave by the water, do whatever you must do to keep the figure contained, and to ensure it doesn't end up in the wrong hands. I don't mean to trouble you or scare you, but the thought of something happening to you without me there makes my blood run cold.

You write that I am "not normal", I think I'm starting to believe you. They tell me my skills are incumbent to the cause, but I'm starting to just feel exhausted. Though, if my exploitation means a quicker return home to you and mother, and an end to this suffering cold, I will do what I must.

It saddens me to think of the selling of mother's ring, but if you must do so to feed yourself, do it without thinking.

I miss you greatly, and I hope for my speedy return. I will go first to the old oak tree. I still remember that snake, how scared we were, how helpless I felt in protecting you. Two heads and twice as angry as it was justified in being. I remember you telling me it was a herald, whereas I thought it was a creature who was dealt an unfortunate hand.

Maybe we were both right.

Stay safe, stay smart, I love you and miss you more with each day that passes,

Calum

Calum

Your letter has found me.... Too late, I fear. I was able to squirrel the parchment out from the statuette, and with no damage to the figure itself, though I find myself wondering if I myself am damaged now. Mother is gone, she slipped away quietly, as she deserved, before I received your missive, and now I believe that is for the best. This artifact has a power that has changed me, awakened hunger deep inside that prior to two weeks ago I dared not acknowledge. You should not come back, they are hunting your kind now, but I will work my way to you-though I fear there will be a cost.

I can see them now. They live in the shadows between buildings and in the darkness under our beds. The church was right to lie to us and tell us everything was fine. The university was right to tell us to trust science and progress and not the prehensile tingling in the stem of our brains that screamed at us that we are not alone. I know now that we truly are not alone. I can see them now, that was father's curse and now it is mine. I pray it will never be yours.

I know how to find them. I know how to hurt them. But they are legion and I am one. When we are together again we will make a plan and try to end this madness, but until then stay safe, stay sane, and know that I love you and that we are the last two that are left.

I will work my way to the market off the King's Road where we saw the juggler catch on fire. I will meet you across the street from the inn we stayed in-approximately two weeks from today.

Love,

A

A,

I'm grateful for your words, I'm sitting reading them beneath my flickering oil lamp, the one father gave me. The flickers remind me of shaking, shivering, as if the lamp fears the darkness you've described. I am sorry to hear about mother, even more so that it was just you alone with her, though your words concern me greatly, so much so I can't properly mourn the loss of our mother. They bring a brazen chill like a winter wind. I've always had a feeling I'm being watched, but the fact that you claim you can see them frightens me. Do not panic, our father bore the sight for many years, I just wish he had told us how. I will help you figure it out. I'll sneak out of camp tomorrow. They need my talents but I'm afraid I don't have much left to give, especially if I know my dear sister is in peril.

I will come to the market just like you said, I remember it fondly, the screaming crowd, the gravely innkeeper, us laughing so hard we nearly fell. It feels like another lifetime entirely, memories that I haven't even lived.

I will be there in two weeks on the dot, if you haven't arrived I will wait for two days in the beaten down inn across the street. You do the same. If one of us hasn't arrived by the allotted time, it means something has gone awfully wrong, and the other must run and never look back.

I pray these aren't my final words to you, but if they are, know my love for you is eternal, and I will hold those memories of our laughter close in my heart forever, wherever I may end up.

I remain, your loving brother,

Calum

Calum—

I saw you today from my cell in the keep. You were being escorted across the bridge by two large men in masks like wolves. Your face was bruised and bloody. I fear we will be reunited soon, though not as we planned it. I have hidden the statue, they will never find it. It is unlikely that anyone will find it. I have no way to get this letter to you, but I wanted you to have proof that my last thoughts were of you.

Stay strong,

A

Five Completed Paintings of My Favorite Places to Ski (Sand Clown "Carletta") by Ander Monson

Listen: that's how they keep you there: so called "ski vacations" and paintings of "her favorite places to ski." *Your* favorite places to ski. Sometimes I imagine you hear me, which is why I say out loud that I know a cover story when I see one, and this is paper thin. Sand clown my ass. Where are your skis, Carletta? Where are your painting supplies? They're not inside the box.

All that space outside of the city to hide in—all those clouds of snow or maybe blowing dust, like the kind summoned by a genie after wishing for a storm—and someone brought you here. Boxed. Kept. I'd say *caged* but you don't seem to think it so. I don't know why I am drawn to you and you alone. The nights are long. I stare through the plastic, working after-hours at the doll factory. If I position myself right I can look at you and see my face, which looks like it is painted too. I know one of our mouths moves, but whose?

My mother said this wasn't a job I would keep long but look who's celebrating her ten years of service to Classic Treasures Industries Incorporated: A Subsidiary of Lisa Frank Incorporated just this week, and look who's not alive anymore, *mom*. One is me, the other's you.

If no one's there and the security cameras are turned away, I talk to you inside your box because it's there, Carletta, because you're there, Carletta, also, I realize saying this, my mom's name before she changed her name to Sandy Alex G. It feels good to say I always resented you, Carletta, Sandy, Alex, G. The way you intruded into my life, how every shape in my life was pressed at least a little to the side by your theories and delusions, the force of being around you, a gravity. The minimizing years. In which: I got flat. In which: I got small. In which I learned to live that way, secondary I mean. The flatness—stillness—is the way. The nail that sticks up gets hammered down or possibly just shoved aside then hammered down into the board and you keep on hammering until the wood is bruised. Maybe you smash your thumb holding the nail or maybe you don't; either way you're dull and bent. Listen: I made a life of this. I know you wouldn't say it's much of one. Night shifts, coming out of the halogen hallways into the early morning nearlight as the smokestacks choke the interstate. They chug steam all night all along the roads. They stop at sunrise when the living wake. At least they say it's just steam, but why then does it smell like maple syrup, cotton cream? Why does it coat my skin when I walk home, following the line of artificial lights, and by the time I get there I feel like I'm getting stiffer, more plastic, by the second.

I know why you won't speak. Some nights when I walk home I get to see into the windows of Animal Sciences I and Animal Sciences II from the elevated path. I don't need to tell you nothing good happens there: it's not like they're curing cow cancer or reducing suffering in any way but on the packaging. It's not like the home for broken dolls, as we call the back room underneath the storage wing. At least when things go there they come out fixed. I mean they must fix things there; where else does the broken go?

Plus the job is easy, mom: I'm just there to look, paid to walk around, paid to be the only thing that walks around at night. Keep what's in the boxes in the boxes. Keep the others out. Keep the shrinkage to an acceptable level appropriate to report. Good nights are those where I'm all I see. There are other nights but we don't have to talk about those.

I told you, mom: it's where I could afford and it's where I chose to stay. I work only ten minutes away. I didn't believe what they said about the power lines and the residue I brought to your home before you were too sick to object. Still when I hear the hum, I close my eyes, and think of you and the manifesto you gave me when I turned ten. A hundred points, a hundred parables, a hundred theories about the world and how it came down on you all your life. I'll admit: a few of them you turned out to be right. Not a lot but enough to make me think, after you had died, what if. If I smoked a pipe I would do so in the window and hold my chin and say out loud WHAT IF.

I don't. Besides there is no smoking anywhere in the building. This is important. They tell you this on day 1. The owner is asthmatic is what I heard but I've never seen the guy so I can't say. To keep it frosty sometimes I walk the hallways in a mask. A venetian clown, I think. I looked it up. A mask I bought at a halloween store. No one else is up except every three days someone comes down from the management wing to take a piss. They say it exactly like this. Their bathroom's better than ours, of course, but sometimes it's engaged (their term) or maybe they just want to sneak a smoke between the security cams. I only assume that no one is watching the security tapes or they'd ask me about the mask. That means they are on for something else. I don't know yet what.

If I stay still, like looking at Carletta in her box, I'm pretty sure I can't be seen. The lights switch off after ninety seconds and start to click click click click off, one after another down the hallway into nothingness. It's the dreaming hours. Management walks on by when they see me. I stand there like a post. Sometimes I salute and hold the pose. I don't breathe, even, as they move. Usually they're in some state of duress by the time they get in here. Management, I mean. If they look anywhere they look over their shoulder, like they're being hunted, as they hustle to the elevator and mash the Going Up button. Is anyone down here they ask, their voice echoing down the hallway and back again. Is there anybody here?

If I said yes I might have to do something I don't want to do so I don't say yes. I've learned a lot. The guy who shot up the place, it's always a guy. This was a long time ago. He didn't even have the right warehouse. He thought that we were Lisa Frank Industries. They're just down the street, I would have said if he would have asked, if I were on duty that night, if I'd had my gun. None of these things occurred. We are just the subsidiary. No one even works here. No one walks the halls alone. Sometimes I'm not sure if they're keeping people out and away from Lisa Frank or if they're trying to keep her in.

I'd be lying if I didn't say I cased the place from time to time, like Animal Sciences II, the more accessible of the two, to see if I could have done better than that guy did, just theoretically, you know, the kind of game you play when you're a kid, like 99 Ways to Die, some bit on some radio show we overheard where they ranked how bad all the ways to die would be, all 99 of them I guess, but I don't know that we ever got past five, not really. We came up with a list and argued over them, the six of us, we were friends then, my mom didn't like any of you but she never had any imagination and so she ended up where she did and that's what's up and that is that. She thought you were trouble and you were, 99 ways to die notwithstanding.

I mean isn't it obvious I took you home, Carletta? I don't know how to ski. I'm from a snowy state. My mom was risk averse. You look a little like her. As a kid I mean, you look like my mom when she was a kid, when she still looked cute in the clown costumes she always wore to remind us how she once trained at clown school before she met your dad, who made her Serious, who got her Down and she stayed Down for the remainder of her life.

Maybe that's why I was drawn to you in your plastic case, or is it me in the plastic case looking out at you? Is it weird to think about kissing your mouth? That there might be something inside you I couldn't think of? I Xrayed all of the dolls one by one to make sure that they didn't have anything that might hurt anyone else. What could be inside a doll that could be a threat to us, I wondered, but needed to be sure. I protected you I mean, the all of you who buy dolls like this, the all of you who are dolls like this. You need me on that wall. You need to buy this doll. Am I me or am I something else? If I can't trust what I see what is the point of seeing? If memory isn't what it is supposed to be how do we even know that we are us? I'm not sure what I'm supposed to do with all these memories of skis.

SONY
CD/DVD PLAYER DVP-SR210P

CD/DVD Player with Remote by Rodrigo Restrepo Montoya

There isn't one corner of this earth that can't be mined. Not one metal, not one need, not one thing. Not one person, either. It's happened to you and it's happened to me.

It had been a long February when I was kindly offered a simple task (this one). I accepted. I had precisely five dollars to donate and was in dire need of a good deed. You see, I'd devoted most of my month to the scriptures of our times (justice.gov/epstein). Entire days and nights at my desk, digging. Flight logs, nicknames, addresses. Dates, routing numbers, shell companies. Friends, murders, invitation lists. Hedge funds, law firms, non-profits. Transcripts, county records, first-person accounts. One afternoon, my wife took a photo of me working at my computer without me knowing. She showed it to me when we sat down for dinner in front of the TV, on the couch. There I was, at my desk, wearing the same face of the bearded Soviet peasant in that photo taken a hundred years ago—the one in which girl, woman, and man listen to the radio for the first time: the daughter on the left, curious, the mother in the middle, disturbed, the father on the right, hollowed-out.

Everybody encounters the abyss from time to time, just as the abyss encounters us—miraculously, disastrously, the gamut, etcetera.

A friend of a friend once showed me a painting he'd made of his favorite parking lot: a cold midwestern sun rising over five or six empty chain stores, the light reflecting faintly off the asphalt grid. It was an emotional painting. I told him that. I asked him why he painted that parking lot specifically. It's where I worked at the time, he said. He had since moved to Utah to study acupuncture. Last I heard, he's married, certified, and practicing.

I, too, am married, certified, and practicing. Commissioned, even, with five dollars to invest in the consensus betterment of our shared reality. I, too, have turned to my favorite parking lot for answers, the completionist one between the edge of town and the foot of the mountain. Gas station. Tire shop. Drive-thru Mexican. Pizza and beer. Dairy Queen. Library. Sheriff's Department. Bank.

Church. James 410 Guns & Ammo. Charter School. Pie shop. Vet clinic. Nail salon. Real estate consultancy. Navajo rug appraisal. Climbing gym (I knew a route-setter there, a man who'd recently lost his mentor to route-setting). Goodwill.

I had five dollars and therefore I had options. Yes, I was priced out of the fish tank. I was likewise priced out of the automatic fish feeder. I wandered the aisles, cursing my luck. Both would have made for a wonderful story. I thought about how easy it would be to paint a quick picture of the fish tank from middle school, the one that held thirty baby fish of the same species, including a slightly larger individual that began eating the others, one by one, until it was huge and the others were few. I thought about how I would've ended the story with the detail about Frankie naming that fish Bob Saget. I considered the father-themed mugs, cheap and funny, but was sick of writing about fathers. I sorted through the extension cords, but found they were either too expensive or too short. I found an obviously cursed statuette of an old gray man that cost only two dollars but was way beyond my spiritual price range. The truth is I might've gone in that direction had I not been hexed the year before—a sad development in and of itself, though far more unsettling when one recalls that curses often return to their originators in threes!

I turned to literature! *Hamlet.* Cookbooks. Self-Improvement paperbacks. Bibles. I looked up James 410: "Humble yourselves before the Lord, and he will lift you up." Boring! *Moby-Dick.* Not boring! *The Last Samurai* by Helen DeWitt. My favorite! A psychotherapy book named after that provocative koan: "If you meet the buddha on the road, kill him!" Last but not least: Rachel Dolezal's memoir, *In Full Color: Finding My Place in a Black and White World.* A signed copy! Her new name! Nkechi Amare Diallo! My fellow Tucsonan! Minutes before I couldn't afford an automatic fish feeder; suddenly I was flush with exciting, affordable options. Too many, really. It was impossible to choose. I wanted to write about Ishmael and Ahab and the rhyming natures of ambition and submission. I wanted to write about *The Last Samurai* and the endeavors of pretentiousness; the absurdity of living in a warrior economy; what it means to have and or be a prosperous American child in a devastatingly American world! Like *Moby-Dick,* maybe! In the sense that both depict the magnitudes of our miniature lives—wrought with difficulty and beauty and ardor and discovery and creation and utter despair! I wanted to write about the koan, and the buddha, and the gun store. My options were multiplying by the second, I was drunk with possibilities! I thought: I thought: If I buy the Rachel Dolezal book, I could write everything I have ever wanted to! How many Rachel Dolezals I have encountered! Three, at least! Oh, how these Rachel Dolezals helped me glimpse the depths of the human abyss! Those vantage points were not free! I paid in various ways! More than money! They took my time! My peace! A transaction had taken place without my knowing! A mining! Like when Indiana Jones replaced the golden idol with his sack of nothing! These were a few of my thoughts, at the Goodwill, in the book aisle. I reminded myself: Life is expensive, shut up and pay!

I carried that book with me. I wondered: What would Helen DeWitt do? The answer: Write and plead! I thought about *The Last Samurai* (again, as usual). The ending. The part about "Straight, No Chaser." How we make what we make so as to be understood by the things we are making—whether it is a person or a persona or a book or a noise. I thought about Robin D.G. Kelley's biography of Thelonious Monk (not available at Goodwill): music that is backwards and is not backwards; that makes itself between the melodic and the disquiet, the familiar and the tectonic, the linear and the spherical. I thought about Monk falling into a sinkhole and the several times he collapsed; how there was concern for his health and his mind, but most of all for his hands! I thought about everything Monk was owed and is still owed. I thought about everything Helen DeWitt is still owed. I thought about *Your Name Here* (not available at Goodwill), and Ilya Gridneff, and the interchangeability of tabloid journalism and war reportage. I thought about a novel as both a product of friendship and a technology for friendship and therefore a remedy for suicide! I thought about what constitutes fiction and what governs publishing! I could have cried!

My head and heart were spinning with options and emotions. I thought: What shall I do, what shall I do? I had shopped at that Goodwill four previous times over the course of seven short years.

There I had bought a total of ten high-quality overshirts; the shirts of dead men, I assume; heavy shirts that have kept me warm and will continue doing so for decades more! I was tired of mining the thrift store, excited yet unsatisfied with the cheap magnificent objects I had collected. Enough! I told myself, Go buy a radio and write a simple parable about the photo of those Soviet peasants! Seconds after making my decision, I discovered there were no radios for sale. Not one! Only a CD/DVD player (with remote!) for $4.99. I plugged it into the wall; its green light came on. I thought: It's alive! I thought: This is the bargain I have been searching for all along! I thought: I have made the absolute most of my budget! I thought: I will make the most of this honest work! I returned Rachel Dolezal's *In Full Color: Finding My Place in a Black and White World* to its place on the shelf.

I could've, and probably should've, finished the story there. Maybe one more line would've tied this all up nicely. Something like: I chose the best deal I could find; I maxed out my budget, and like always, I kept the receipt!

You might be thinking: He's trying way too hard to make a point with this piece. To which I might say: Well, yes, I am! Many! Even if I have been unimaginative, even if I have been rather foolish, even if I have sacrificed virtuosity for verisimilitude, I have tried to make some sense of this simple task!

I'm just about done here. Two last things:

One: You could take a photo of someone seeing the photo of those three Russian peasants listening to the radio for the first time and you just might see said person make the same expression as one of those three Russian peasants.

Two: I present to you a CD/DVD player that can help one encounter, approximate, and experience the miraculousness of life from a safe and comfortable distance! I present to you a remote with which one can shake hands with the world!

Oh, and what if there is no safe distance? And what if one can't shake hands with the world?

8 908019 403343
2.00 in x 5.00 in (5.08 cm x 12.70 cm)
Distributed By:
Radiaant Expovision Pvt. Ltd
A-70, Sector- 64, Noida, Uttar Pradesh
Origin- India
F16837774 Q4/2025
Age 3+
$3
All new materials
FIBER FILL - 100% Polye
Reg. No. PA-19616 (IN)
F16837774 Q4/2025
Spot Clean only

Train/End (Carrot Keychain) by Matthew Morris

> Once, I boarded a train; leaving my home,
> I watched the red sky, the low sun glowing—
> an ember I could blow into flame...
> —Natasha Trethewey, "(Self) Portrait"

There is no finer vegetable than a carrot, you've said, to pull full-bodied from the [riven, fecund] earth. And when we part as lovers, when our text messages cease to carry flaming red or arrowed pink hearts or that blue soup bowl come from the language we devised, the carrot takes everything else's place; it means we're rooting for each other: I for you, you for me. Once, I boarded a train, Trethewey wrote in that poem from Bellocq's Ophelia, early, which you read with me, and once, you know, we did this, too (boarded), the low sun holding the faintest, most promising of light, for/though neither of us'd been with anyone in some time. Once, I told you that I am entranced by once-as-clause. Once, before the (romantic) love came undone, was uprooted, so that I could see more clearly again, seeing as I couldn't anymore, though I was very sorry for that, but not long before I said goodbye to you in that way (there are a great many forms of love, yes/no?): once, before but not long ahead of that breaking, I plucked a carrot keychain from Target's $5-or-less bin, near your first Missouri apartment, in The Tiger Village; then, I bought a pillow that I thought still might be for you, but even if/though it wasn't, I thought you'd want someone else's head resting there someday, because you were, always are rooting for me. I got the memory foam kind: you rest your head against it night after night; the pillow learns your body, adjusts itself to your face, the top of your head, your chin and ears and nose. A carrot keeps sharp the vision, or that's what I was taught, my Black father tucking babies in my paper bag school lunch, and although you no longer fall asleep beside me, our bodies in (such close) orbit, I can see that you're/we're not leaving, that you'll still be a figure in my life and I in yours, all I've ever wanted from a breakup being for the connection not to be severed wholly, for my companion-in-life to still be part of it. (I hear in my head Lucy Dacus: May I still play …) This weekend you're with your best friend, a couple of hours west, tasting cheeses at Green Dirt Farms, and I'm figuring out which tchotchkes ought to stay on my shelves, which belong in a box (forever?): the shell you brought me from Normandy, where your vision five-minutes splintered but then came back whole; a miniature candle in the shape of a saguaro, whose waxen sturdiness I won't burn; miniature fragile-as/because-glass birds, one blue and white with a long, sharp bill, the other a bright yellow, red, green. A mutual friend tells me that I'm family to him and his wife and their very young daughter and that you are, too, and that if we can be friends, it will be best for the others; I know straightaway that he's right but that the goodwill can't be about anyone else, has to start with you and me. I get up on the fencing behind City of Refuge, look out over our modest downtown: the Jesse Hall rotunda, the shops along Walnut and Broadway, some of them in Sharp's End, the Black business district, once and now again. (What street's that Italian place we went to, Endwell? We split salad and pizza; you wore a black dress—) I put my hands before the embers of our slow-shifting love, only now remember the bellows a friend and his bald father would use to stoke a fire on Virgina winter afternoons, after school, the sixth or seventh grade: when I think of you, I am not angry, devastated, guilty, or rootless; no, and/but I still want so much for (each of) us.

Wine Bottle Painted to Look Like a Woman by Aidan Murray

Ava Perryman looked in the mirror as she finished getting ready. She was nervous and felt it bubbling in her stomach. She knew she looked good, a little heavier than she would have liked, but she was confident in what she saw and was confident that he would like it too. She ran her fingers through her dark hair and double checked her make up. She wore a baby blue dress that contrasted against her dark skin. She swayed it left to right and watched it twirl. She gave thanks to God for his wonderful timing, locked her apartment door, grabbed an umbrella, and walked down the stairs. She did not think that it would rain, but it was cloudy and nothing was going to stop her from getting what she wanted.

He had come up to Ava on the street while she was walking home from work two weeks earlier. She was usually hesitant of anyone coming up to her, but something about the way his blue eyes sparkled in the light of the setting sun. It was as if he had put her under a spell.

Part of it was his eyes. They shined like they had been carved out of crystal or polished glass. Like someone had cut them to exact, divine specifications and then polished them until shone with an almost artificial glow. When he looked at him it felt like he could see inside her and it filled her with warmth and comfort.

He had told her she was beautiful and his appreciation of her after a full day at the restaurant had made her feel special and safe. He told her about her own restaurant and how she would be a great fit there. He was charming, handsome, and most of all, white. She had no idea why he had chosen her but she was grateful that he did and knew that God had something to do with it. Two potential opportunities had been given to her by Him, which in her desperate state, she knew she needed.

Ava assumed he was rich, not just because he was white, but also because he owned his own telephone and his own restaurant. She did not want him to think that's all she wanted. That was part of it for her obviously, but she also appreciated how safe he made her feel, how much it felt like he cared. He had walked her home and left her with his phone number. It was like he had cast a spell that made the rest of the world disappear as they talked the night away. Her short walk home had felt even shorter than usual and she did not glance around once on the streets where she normally would. When he left she felt an ache, a craving, She needed to see him once more.

Ava had called him the next day as soon as she got off work the next day and found a payphone. The two of them talked for over an hour. They talked and he had asked her on a date at his restaurant the following week, Friday, at seven pm. They lingered on the phone until well past the last light left the sky. On her way home it was all she could think about and again she didn't glance around knowing she was safe and that God had for sure given her this opportunity. She spent the entire week and a half looking forward to their date and finally, it had arrived.

Ava walked down the street and looked up at the restaurant he told her to meet him at. It was fancier than she expected and saw even fancier people sitting inside laughing and enjoying themselves. There was a small porch where two couples and two families sat at wooden tables built from wine barrels and ate food that looked to be prepared with excruciating, calculated, accuracy. White couples and white families she thought, but strangely the thought did not fill her with dread. She stood and stared for a moment, imagining the possibilities.

She would love to work here, she thought, she longed to be a part of this world, a part of a class in which she never felt she would belong. The opportunity was at her fingertips and for the first time in her life her all apprehension was gone. It was as if something inside her had replaced her usual doubts with confidence and optimism. She could imagine the two of them holding hands as they welcomed the first guests of the night and then later again as they said farewell to the last calls. She would love to own this place, she corrected herself, to make herself a part of it.

Ava walked around the back of the restaurant to a small black door with a metal grate as he told her to do. She knocked on it three times, again, like he'd instructed. A moment later the door opened and there he was. He smiled at her and motioned for her to follow him down the stairs. When she looked into his sparkling blue eyes she could no longer see anything else.

Ava followed him inside and looked around. They entered a cellar where the only source of light was a few small candles scattered about the large shelves stacked high with bottles of wine. To her surprise there was a warmth coming from the bottom of the stairs. She felt it grow and overtake her as she walked down the steps. It felt familiar, it soon would be, she thought.

She saw a table in the middle of the room with a labelless bottle of wine in the middle and two cups. She glanced around and noticed that each bottle of wine on the shelves had a handpainted label of a beautiful woman on it.

"I thought we could have more privacy down here," he said to her, continuing to smile. "I wanted to spend the evening just focusing on you, and how we can best bring a part of you into the restaurant."

"I was thinking the same thing," She replied, "I love that you chose this place, it's perfect."

He pulled out one of the chairs and offered for Ava to take a seat. She smiled back at him, curtsied, and sat down. He poured her a glass of wine from the unmarked bottle. She watched the purple liquid as it filled the glass for the moment and then turned back to look at him as he sat down.

"I told my chefs to bring down our dinner personally in a half hour, is that okay? I thought that would give us time to catch up. I told them to make their favorite dishes."

"Yes, that sounds wonderful," Ava said once again looking at his eyes, again transfixed.

She pulled out of the trance for a moment and forced herself to take a sip of wine. She can't be creepy, she thought. She didn't want to ruin this moment for herself, this opportunity. She asked God for help but began struggling with the words. They started to jumble together in her head. God I offer mseylf to- She looked back at him and he started to look further and further away. As her vision grew fuzzy and faded to black she could still see his blue eyes piercing through the darkness.

Ava Perryman wakes up. She looks down and now she's watching their date from a third person perspective. She watches herself as she laughs. How he smiles and his blue eyes twinkle like he just told a joke. Then she notices that his date is not with her, it is in fact a completely different woman sitting next to him. She frowns. She tries to move. She notices that she can't. She tries to look down to see what's trapping her but she can't do that either.

For a moment she is confused. She watches the girl pass out and fall over. Impossibly Ava watches as the other girl's body begins to dissolve into a gas and transport itself towards the unlabeled bottle of wine in the middle of the table. Ava tries to move once more, but again she can't. She is trapped on the shelf.

Ava watches, helpless as he gets up and leans over to collect the bottle which is now rocking and shaking slightly. Ava sees that the bottle is no longer unlabeled and instead has a beautiful image of the woman who had just disappeared hand-painted its side. He picks it up and sets it on the shelf right next to her. One by one he blows out the candles and then they are alone in the dark.

She wakes up once again. This time in the light. She looks around and sees a family of white people laughing around a table, eating meatballs and drinking wine. She is moved and poured and moved and poured until she is empty. When she is, she sees him walk towards the table and begin a conversation with the family. She cannot make out the words, like before, all she notices are the eyes.

Dairy

Possible Interdimensional Energy Source Housed in a Die Cast Replica of a Milk Truck (Possible Cargo Cult Fetish?) (Hot Wheels Dairy Truck) by David Mutschler

Good day potential bidders,

It is I, intrepid explorer and merchant Dr. Divad Relhcstum, and I can no longer keep this item as it may hold some unobtanium material that I also feel is above my pay grade. Being devoid of children, and as an avid reseller of curiosities, oddities, and artifacts from around the world, yours truly has spent years combing the small markets from various locales, and I can tell you personally that I truly have never seen an object quite like this!

Acquired from the glass cabinet of a Thrift-N-Save, this beautiful relic of a time past can be yours—if you dare! Marked "Dairy," this miniature truck is no doubt the fastest way to a soft serve this side of the Mississippi. Highly modified, this simulacrum of the ancient past has eight, count them, eight exhaust pipes, and translucent blue unobtanium energy sources that would look more at home in a time traveling DeLorean than your local ice cream purveyor. This extreme drive train conducts its roaring fury into the custom rear wheels that have been engineered to withstand the horsepower expected with such an unusual and perhaps interdimensional power source. As a strange, and perhaps mystical or ceremonial, object the makers would have been familiar with; we can only speculate as to what the original creators of this object were trying to portray outside of the familiar archaeological record. Making this find even more unique is the makers marks found on the underside. "Chill Mill", "1186 MJ. 1. NL.", "Hot Wheels", "H 0 3" are all to be found on the bottom alongside an exciting mark which speaks to the exotic providence of the item:

"Made in Malaysia".

Was it used in some cargo cult by indigenous islanders? Was it owned by a sorcerer of ill repute in the archipelago? We don't know, BUT IT MAY HAVE BEEN!! Cargo cults flourished after the end of World War II when indigenous islanders in the south pacific deified the technologically superior military apparatus of the European and American allies. The "cargo" was usually canned foods brought in by soldiers and airmen and other luxuries. Believing the cargo would keep coming, and ignorant of the end of the second great war, many isolated tribes would build full size effigies of planes and Jeeps. Burning and clearing land to make airstrips for the divine gods to return upon causing great ecological damage. Others would create miniatures, or fetishes, of these vehicles in the hopes it would entice the ancestor and cargo deity to send more supplies. This led to a collapse of social and religious constructs on many of these islands as the limited resources would be used for these endeavors instead of traditional lifeways. The exclusion of headlights lends itself to this interpretation, as peoples in industrialized nations would have been aware of the need of such fixtures meanwhile a traditional society would be ignorant of the stylistic representations present in western society.

More details of its providence can be found from the words of the purveyor of fine goods it was purchased from, a gentleman who goes by the name of "Derrick":

"Yeah, I knew it was something special the moment Nyoman came in. Usually we are donation only, but I knew this was special and Nyoman told me he needed money for milk, so I gave him some gold coins to go pawn in exchange for it. He had tears coming down his eyes when he let it go, like he just gave away his first born. And I tell you, I have just never seen anything like it outside of a Michael J. Fox and Christopher Lloyd film- and I've seen all of them! Later I had some shifty looking, and what I can only assume to be, Libyan rebels come in asking about "milk". That is when I knew this was something truly special. What are the odds, right? The wear on the edges of the die-cast model suggests it was handled and inserted into a power source regularly. I know what I have, so I am not accepting any low-ball offers. But I will let it go for less than two dollars, because you seem like a trustworthy guy, and don't want to be wrapped up into any time altering narratives. That is above my pay, and they don't pay me much."

!!!

Do not pass on this once in a lifetime opportunity to own a possibly culturally significant artifact from the storied shores of Malaysia!

Buyer assumes all risks inferred, implied, or otherwise upon the purchase of this item.

PayPal preferred.

No returns.

...Item does not ship to Libya.

All my best, and happy bidding!!!

Sparkly Shoes (Shoe Statue) by L. C. J. Owen

At 17 years old, she got kicked out of her first bar, a Southeastern Michigan Tiki bar called The Flowing Aku-Aku Paradise, because of her shoes. Leaving the bar bathroom, she tripped over her sparkly red platforms, landed on the floor, and was informed by the bartender that she had to leave.

In an irony, she had not only successfully entered the bar on a fake ID but also had yet to have a drink. Still, the fall on 3-inch heels had been spectacular enough to convey excessive drunkenness, a fact that made her a little proud.

A request to let her friends further inside know was denied by bartender and security alike — probably sensible as they feared this was just an excuse to disappear back into the bar's deepening tiki twilight, the establishment a warren of fake bamboo screens, concealing groups, huddling in circles, drinking from shared bowls of the bar's signature, giant blood-red drink, the supposedly Polynesian Tarantula Twist!

But her purse was with her friends, so without phone or wallet, all she could do was sit outside, butt on curb's edge, and wait for one of them to notice she was gone.

And that was where she met Wolf Spider (not his given name), lead singer of the fantasy-death metal band Sickening Radiance.

Not that she knew who he was at the time. Shorn of the story of his music, he just seemed like a short, skinny middle-aged guy with stringy hair. He did seem disappointed she didn't know who he was, dropping references to a song a lot of people your age seem to like. Later she was to realize that this was The Dark and Sticky Sacrifice of Love, an uncharacteristically slow tempo'd track of Sickening Radiance that was, indeed, periodically popular with teenagers. It was slow and balladic and the lyrics seemed on the surface romantic, crooning about sacrificing everything for love. By contrast, the rest of SR's oeuvre was more traditional metal; a lot of the group's iconography centered on Fenriz, a supernatural wolf-creature that was kind of the Norse wolf-figure Fenrir, foretold to herald the end of the world, and kind of not—most of Sickening Radiance's lyrics were about Fenriz breaking his chains, eating people, sometimes growing Cerberus-like extra heads, and being generally awesome and apocalyptic. Dark and Sticky was the only track that might be called romantic.

At the time, Wolf Spider had a fleck of potato chip at the edge of his lip. She kept on being distracted from the conversation, wondering if the next time Wolf Spider put a menthol cigarette to his mouth, if the potato-piece would finally dislodge. She kept wanting to tell him about it but didn't. The moment was never right and Wolf Spider didn't pause much while talking.

Later, she wondered if Wolf Spider had wiped the small crumb from his mouth, or if he had not, unappealing, lit one cigarette with another and referred to it as buttfucking, if her whole future might have been different.

He had just asked her to go back to his rental house, which was only a few blocks away, to listen to some records, when a friend finally appeared, out of the bar's doors. "There you are!"

At this point, a choice: but it wasn't one, really. She'd felt Schrodinger's attraction—it existed and it didn't exist at the same, it flickered when for a moment when his face was lit up in a menthol glow, and then faded when he didn't let her finish a sentence, but the presence of an observer collapsed the delicate fluctuation of desire and repulsion: of course she was going with her friends.

"Eh, it's fine, definitely not a virgin anyway," she heard Wolf Spider mutter, as she left him, in a tone of knowing dismissal. As it happened, this wasn't technically true—but it felt true in the moment, and damning.

Twenty years later, The Dark and Sticky Sacrifice of Love went viral on TikTok, and then, a little bit later, on Instagram Reels, which she scrolled through while pregnant with and then nursing her first baby.

The chorus Sacrifice everything for looooooove….no sacrifice is too great for loooooooovee meant that it was in the background of a lot of couple-videos or couple-plus-newborn baby, or look at my baby all grown up-type videos. But it turned out the rest of the lyrics were quite violent, the narrative of the song being about a literal blood-sacrifice, so it was weird to watch people demonstrate noodle recipes or pelvic-floor exercises while snippets of the non-chorus played in the background: blood gushes down, the virgin viscera spills abound, knife plunging into your bosom and you swoooooooon wailed Wolf Spider as someone chopped garlic or did squats or kissed their baby.

She told the story too much, to friends and family and work colleagues. "I've only ever been kicked out of a bar once…." and then the fondly-impatient look that meant you were definitely repeating yourself: "…And you weren't even drunk, I know."

In honor of her story, her husband bought her a plasticine statuette of a red sparkly platform, a single vessel that could theoretically hold a bottle of wine but never did. It sat on a shelf in their room, a sort-of shoe, alone and forever unmated. Like her and her well-worn story, it was a simulacra—almost exciting, but not.

For a long time, Wolf Spider was her celebrity story, her fun-fact at ice breakers. But as she googled him more, she wondered if she should stop bringing him up. There was never any formal allegations or charges, but rumors and rumored accusations periodically circulated online, usually regarding underage girls. She'd always thought her fake ID made the story less creepy—why would he have any reason to believe she wasn't 21?— but now she wondered. As her kids got older, and she got less sleep and got more anxious, staying up late and googling all the terrible possibilities of the world, it was hard not to descend down internet-holes about Wolf Spider.

For example: his solo work. After a bitter split with Sickening Radiance, Wolf Spider enjoyed a little bit of solo success, buoyed by his old song going viral. I killed you in your red shoes and it was romantic had some niche success, off the album What's in the basement, supported on the Withered Corpse Tour.

Paranoia, to believe you were reading coded messages in song lyrics. Fantasy-death metal was not autobiographical. It was fantasy! It was right there in the name! It was all about mythology and metaphor.

Presumptuous, to think there had been a moment, a split decision, between you and something dark, or even noteworthy—that you played some part in an iconography of terror. People always wanted to feel close to a disaster, to have had a near-escape from death or a profound encounter with a celebrity. The reality was a creep with a crumb mouth who had long forgotten you. But it did not seem so when Wolf Spider died. Everyone talked about what they found in his L.A. compound. Among the finds: a room full of pairs and pairs of sparkly red shoes.

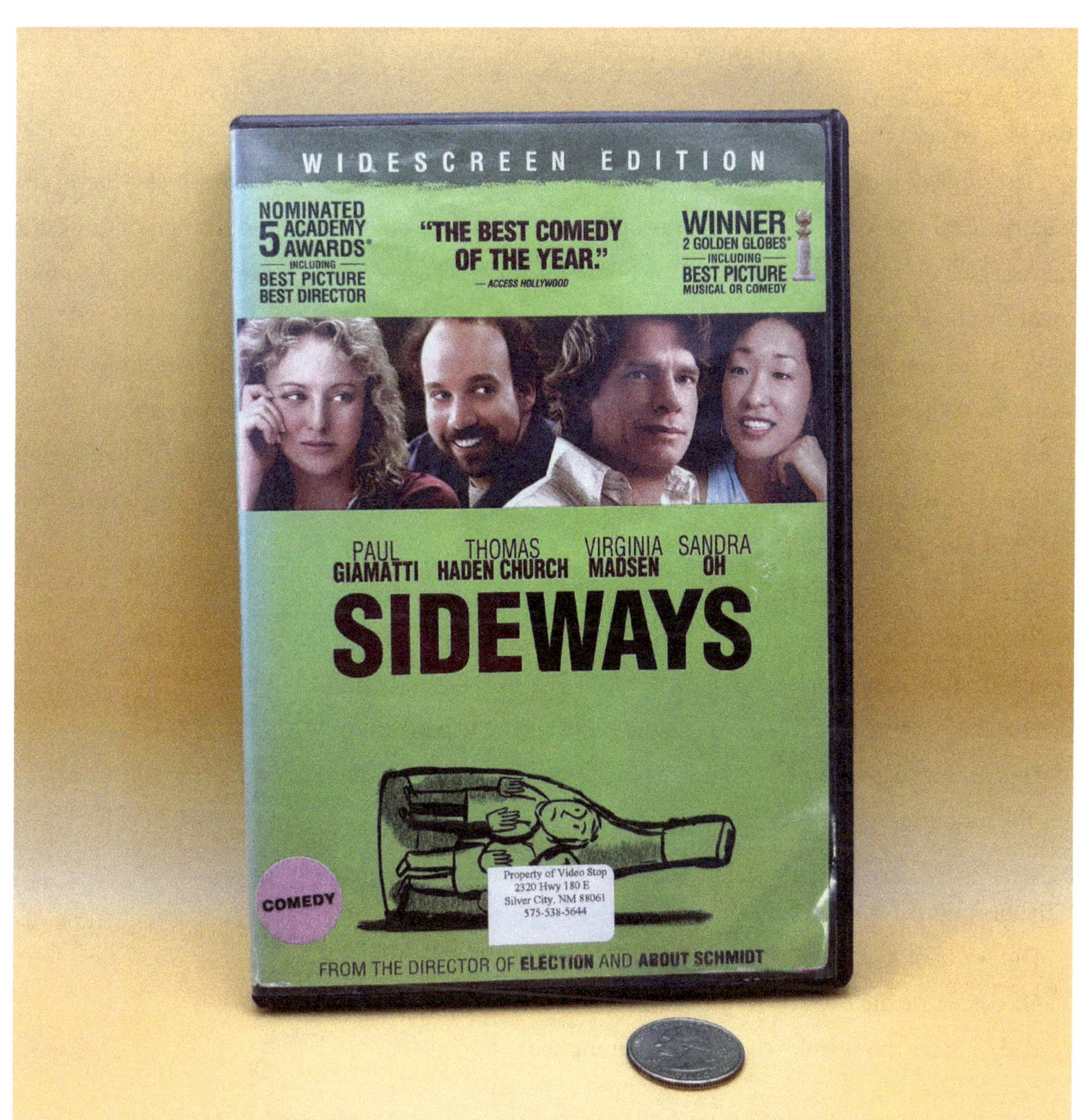
WIDESCREEN EDITION
NOMINATED 5 ACADEMY AWARDS® INCLUDING BEST PICTURE BEST DIRECTOR
"THE BEST COMEDY OF THE YEAR."
— ACCESS HOLLYWOOD
WINNER 2 GOLDEN GLOBES® INCLUDING BEST PICTURE MUSICAL OR COMEDY
PAUL GIAMATTI
THOMAS HADEN CHURCH
VIRGINIA MADSEN
SANDRA OH
SIDEWAYS
COMEDY
Property of Video Stop
2320 Hwy 180 E
Silver City, NM 88061
575-538-5644
FROM THE DIRECTOR OF ELECTION AND ABOUT SCHMIDT

Bouquet (Sideways DVD) by Lydia Paar

Working in customer service is mostly thankless, which is why so many of us drink.

Occasionally, though, it brings magic, like when you get to sneak through the secret cellar of the historic hotel where John Dillinger was once caught, then through it out into the labyrinth of dirt tunnels below a main artery of downtown Tucson, just because you knew a manager during a moment that he also may have been drinking.

We'll call him Jim, and Tim worked with him at the fancy restaurant adjacent to the hotel, under the same ownership, where Jim was the somme and Tim managed bar. Jim toured us through the hotel's basement and sub-basement, where a bunch of rags had spontaneously combusted earlier that month, then onto the roof where you could see they were storing far too much construction material, likely leftover from an earlier fire.

What the building ablaze with Dillinger in it? I couldn't recall.

But nonetheless, magic: history and the present all connected up as if through tunnels. Time slides sideways, unimportant.

One day, Josh said to Tim that he had a Napa tasting trip planned.

He'd arranged to tour a few different wineries with the idea of ordering more of the wines he liked for the restaurant.

"The tastings will all be free."

Did we want to come?

Of course we did.

Did we have the airmiles to get to San Francisco?

Somehow, we did.

So we took a long weekend in February and went. Shoulder season. Not tourist season. Not harvest time. The winery owners might actually have a moment to schmooze.

As we flew through NorCal's moody clouds, then drove our rental car out past city structures and moody woods until the un-treed hills began to roll around us, I remembered the surreal feeling of watching the well-known 2004 movie on the same subject, and in the same region, *Sideways*.

You know: the "I am not drinking any *fucking Merlot!" Sideways*.

Steals from his mom, and cosigns his engaged friend's cheaterly habits *Sideways*.

Writes forever, finishes never.

It's a romp.

The first time I saw it, I was tenderly twenty-one, and I remember wondering why people would bother to travel for wine, because I'd only had the bottles my misbehaving friends and I had shoulder-tapped from gas stations previously, which puckered my stomach.

As I grew into an older, and of course, stereotypically calmer Oregonian, I traded in my shoulder-tapped beer, and then eventually my legally-bought vodka and late-night club dancefloors for the soft comfort of a wide array of Willamette Valleys pinots, which I could sit and sip with a friend or two on a back porch and talk…some method of mind-bending that made me feel a fraction more financially secure and a tad bit creatively clear, and able, in rainy evenings, to lose track of time in a leisurely, rather than a manic manner.

Soon, I thought, we'd be out there where they made the stuff, all kinds of it: driving through the quiet, letting eons of human history and effort unfurl into reflection on our tongues (our eager, eager tongues). Normally, we'd be on the backside of the bar pouring samples with Sandra Oh, or serving up absorbent victuals with Virginia Madsen, but this time, we were the customers. In fact, more than that.

Our first stop was our sleeping quarters, at a well-appointed loft in downtown Napa connected to a tasting room. They gave us all hearty pours, and they were good, and they talked about their business, and I then was drunk.

We slept easy and awoke the next day, ready to work, a tricky day of pacing our consumption and trying to sound smart about grapes. We had to take as much into our minds and memories as into our guts. I have no recollection of breakfast. But then we were off: we had to make 2-3 wineries per day to get through all of Jim's appointments.

The first place was an enormous Illuminati-type compound with steel casks stacked by the hundred into giant well-secured rooms, scientists in a lab measuring the minutiae of pH, yeast, and heat, and a private hosting room with a huge oak table overlooking the grounds. The well-dressed vineyard rep walked us through the history of each varietal they carried at this table, all so perfect I knew I could never afford to return.

Jim bought a bottle. We demurred, but took the list to "order later."

Then we went to a castle, where we were given a quiz about vintage, and Tim beat Jim the somme.

We went to a scrubby but fine little farm where they only made three kinds of red.

Then a kind of mega-cabin on a mountain.

At one spot, all right angles and concrete, I read the list price wrong in a bath of golden sunlight and spent $100 on a zin.

We learned that according to some estimates, American merlot farmers lost $400 million in the first few years after Sideways.

Then we drank some merlot and loved it.

One late evening, we still had to eat, so we went French, and put the equivalent of rent on credit, because it was open and gorgeous and when would we ever do this again?

Half the time, unlike our European drinking peers, we didn't have healthcare.

So then we slept in more, the sleepiness accumulating. We arose and schmoozed again.

We decanted. We swirled. We nudged our noses deep into bouquets.

We got heady.

"Yes, it's zesty!"

"Look at those legs!"

We wondered together how to find your legs as a newly-minted vintner, to root in this peculiar noble world of rot and must that crossed the ancient at home and abroad: deep history, which also seemed to hold a future, financially, and as a major part of the current cultural zeitgeist.

You could definitely lose decades in this maze of detail, in a mostly-velvet relaxation punctuated by notable seasonal stress: Would it burn? Would it blight?

You hate the tourists, but you need them to survive etc. etc.

The only insight into the mystery I was able to scrabble together was that I wanted more of it. The magic, the chewy sense of time, slowed-down and swishy and stretched.

Three years to start.

Several million dollars worth of labor and materials to coax a ripening.

And then begin again, another process with glass, with pressure, and eventually, public persuasion.

The layers fell around us as onion skin.

But in the end, as in the movie, we simply had to go home again.

Modernity crash-landed with a plane whose engine inhaled a duck, so we waited in the terminal for hours.

We ourselves ripened.

We had some airport chablis, but despite its local sourcing…it soured us.

Eventually, finally, we arrived.

Jim got fired: the hotel/restaurant owners wished they'd gone instead.

Tim quit on principle.

Then we all found other jobs serving other people in different ways, and life went back to its usual baseline.

But for a moment, as if we were John Dillingers or Paul Giamottis ourselves, hoarding and running and burning our way through some secret future hopeful history, it wasn't.

The Silent Instrument (Conductor's Baton) by Dorian Rolston

A few weeks ago, my girlfriend and I went to an estate sale. I'm no particular expert when it comes to assessing the worth of objects, but I consider estate sales a grand indulgence, combing through someone else's possessions for both anything of potential hidden value but also, more importantly, a sense of the life they lived. It's rare that we get to thumb over every little thing; even at a friend's house, while I'm insatiably curious to examine the bookshelf, I find myself painfully aware of how uncouth it might look to pay the library more attention than the gracious host, and I certainly wouldn't dare go onto the kitchenware, garden tools, textiles, and all the knickknacks lined up on the windowsill. I suppose there's a social prohibition against prying that I can't quite seem to break through, as much as I want to open every cabinet door and run my hands along the tapestries. But something happens after a person dies—it releases us, and them, and we can finally give an honest appraisal of our days.

Of course, I didn't know anything about this person who lived at 1127 Decatur St. But that's part of the thrill, trying to reconstruct them out of the contents of the house, what they've left behind. Freud says something similar about the process of psychoanalysis, famously considering himself an archaeologist of sorts. He once compared working with a patient to "excavating a buried city," and as a psychodynamic therapist myself, I have to admit my natural impulse is to dig. There's something about the so-called "presenting problem"—what the person is coming in the door with, what they *think* they need help with—that makes me wonder what treasure might be lying beneath, both in the sense of the site of the original wound and, quite possibly, the most precious psychic material waiting to have the latch broken and the lid pried loose. So off I go, even in my downtime, rummaging through other people's stuff.

We got our first glimpse the night before. Huddled around my laptop in the dark, clicking through

New Orleans listings at EstateSales.NET, we got caught by the "!!30% Off Sunday!!" tagline and clicked, opening a veritable photo album's worth of enticing pics. Scrolling through dozens of shots of the obligatory fine china and forgotten dresser drawers emptied out, at first nothing really registered, not being Wedgewood connoisseurs ourselves. But we were impressed by the sheer amount of things in the drawers: embroidered patches and silk ties, Zippo lighters and old coins. There were red velvet jewelry boxes spilling out with necklaces and rings and bracelets. Exotic-looking figurines of carved elephants and emerald Buddhas processed down the page. I got the impression of a well-travelled man of some discernment, but also a touch of the collector about him, seemingly unable to part with anything and happy for the subsequent miscellany. A great potential psychoanalytic case study.

Meanwhile, in the background, the general look of the place was growing on us. My girlfriend and I have what you might call a *rustic* aesthetic, a fetish for all things crumbly and overgrown and set somewhere charmingly pastoral. (She and a childhood friend came up with the term "gentle crumble," which seems apt both for us and the sinking city.) My ideal house is a stone cottage tucked away in the French countryside, covered with creeping vines, its windows flung open to the elements, chickens and goats coming in and out, fire crackling in the hearth—something out of a Rohmer film. So this seemed pretty close, all considered. The listing warned visitors to "WATCH YOUR STEP" upon entering the old Creole townhouse down an uneven cobblestone alley. Under exposed beams, you appeared to wind your way up three spiral staircases, each with what seemed original hardwood. The loft would require ducking. The main landing, heavily laid with Persian rugs before a red brick hearth, had two sets of French doors opening onto the balcony. A word on French Quarter balconies: you're never sure you want to stand on them, afraid to test your weight on the sinking supports. Charmed.

Just as we were about to start planning our next-day visit, we were stopped dead in our tracks.

After a number of tasteful nudes, mostly oil paintings in gilded frames, along with some fine etchings and black-and-white sketches that might've been drafts of the final composition, there was... Lou Ferrigno, himself oiled-up and muscly, flexing as Hercules in the movie of that name. Next to him, Silverster Stallone, less oily but somehow more smoldering, eyed the camera with his title belt and gloves from *Rocky III*. Finally, the pinup of David Hasselhoff became almost cliché at this point, tufts of Baywatch-era chest hair sprouting from beneath a too-tight leather jacket, grinning boyishly. What were we to make of this interlude—this interlude in the nude?

Perhaps this was a commentary on the human form, drawing connections between the figurework of the Renaissance and today. Lingering on the sinewy, glistening contours of the modern version of the Greek god, I could see a case being made for this Ferrigno being our Michelangelo. But then I thought that maybe we were just going to the home of a gay man with taste, and this pulled from his private collection. But what even *is* taste? And why, for that matter, would sexy-stud movie posters seem to contradict that? Why not mix high and low art—and how to tell the difference? Anyone can like beautiful things, after all, or hire someone to pick them out. Real taste is having a coherent aesthetic irrespective of the rules, something more recognizably you than any particular era or movement. As Phillip Lopate says of the essay form, it's the "soloist's personal signature flowing through the text" that we return for, regardless of content. I believe I saw something of a distinct John Hancock on the walls, and felt I had a lot to learn from this man, whoever he was. I guess that's rather neo-Freudian of me to say, suggesting that the doctor has as much (if not more) to learn as the patient.

I grew up in a household defined by other peoples' tastes. Rather than a consultation with me or my brother, the brutes, on what we liked or disliked, the determining factor seemed to be what would look good in a magazine. It wasn't even to the guests' own liking. My grandmother used to come over regularly for tea, and my mother would serve her quite literally on a silver platter. This old woman with thin lips and fine white hair had escaped wartime Lithuania and eventually fled the USSR for Canada; she wasn't exactly picky. All she ever seemed to want was a cup of Lipton's and to pop a couple of the Mentos she always carried with her in a roll surreptitiously tucked in her purse, smuggled into her daughter's home like Soviet contraband. How I craved those sweet, beaming white discs, like little moons! But out would come the platter and its china teapot and cups and saucers, those shortbreads placed just so—time for high tea. My grandmother always flashed me a mischievous look when it was Mentos time.

Even without company, the house felt staged. The dining chairs were for dining, the armchairs for lounging, and the accent chairs—god forbid you sat or ate in one—just for decoration. We were all made to suffer a borderline psychotic paranoia about "crumbs," constantly searching for them in cushion crevices and in the carpet pile, an ever-present threat we had to keep at bay. Once, I made the mistake of sitting, and indeed eating, in said accent chair. It was a plush yellow, comfy to sink into, with burnished bronze buttons on the arms that I loved to rub. (It was not the first time, admittedly, I had sat and eaten in it.) "Dorian!" I heard the familiar cry, the way a dog might learn to wince at the sound of its own name, meaning trouble. When it was painstakingly pointed out to me how the yellow was losing its lustre, the bronze its sheen, I felt guilty of some unforgivable crime.

Perhaps it was in a moment like this that I turned to my ancestors for guidance. On the walls, hanging in their Rococo frames, oil portraits of fancy-looking people wearing severe expressions watched over me. I both feared and admired them; I worried about the possibilities for punishment at the hands of people of such obvious distinction, liable to have me shipped off to boarding school to be caned, or worse, but then I would console myself with the thought of being similarly blue blood. Surely they wouldn't do such a thing to their own kind, their very kin! Only later did I find out that these were not my ancestors at all, just some anonymous aristocrats. Likely, my mother found them at an estate sale.

How has this affected me, you might wonder. Well, I'm predictably neurotic, bobbing my head like a chicken, full of indecision and lacking any stable core from which to orient myself. To carry the analogy further, I can act like a chicken with his head cut off, at once highly suspicious of the so-called finer things in life and driven mad by the slightest sign that someone's ostentation means they think they're better than me. I have an inferiority complex; the royalty in Rococo frames still look down on me. And it's very hard, if not impossible, to ever know with certainty what I like. But I don't want to give you the wrong idea. I'm not blaming my mother, at least not entirely. She really was, and is, a woman of impeccable taste. I don't know this by way of any aesthetic sensibility of my own, of course. Sadly, I inherited none of that, much to her chagrin. But, as they say, people talk.

To me, she just looks like a blond version of Audrey Hepburn from Breakfast at Tiffany's, a comparison she'd find flattering but to my eyes seems a bit overdressed for the occasion. Others see things differently. Going thrifting, a regular childhood pastime and still a chance for the two of us to bond and reminisce (if somewhat conflicted), I might hear, "That woman—did you see her? Is that a Chanel suit?" I accept the flattery on her behalf. For her part, my mother pretends not to notice, continuing to flick through the racks, intent on the task at hand. That or she's just oblivious to the praise at this point. I suppose they're not saying anything she doesn't already know. When you devote yourself, above all else, to beauty, it comes with something of a Narcissusian bargain: wanting nothing more than to gaze at your own reflection, yet knowing the risk of falling in.

Vanity, of course, like any drug, has ambivalence at its core. We need the hit of validation but simultaneously shy away from it, wishing we didn't. This was my introduction to the world of "second-hand," that magical realm where priceless things could be had at a bargain, only you weren't to tell anyone how you got them. Our regular dealer down the street was a boutique called Extoggery, which we took to calling "Rex Toggieri," after an Italian fashion designer who didn't actually exist.

In my child's mind, I must've wanted the lie to be true so desperately that I took to picturing some pock-faced old Italian man in wraparound shades and an ill-fitting suit, that creepy, all-powerful Rex. Rex wasn't so good to me. Apart from the somewhat forced mother-son bonding ritual, I only ever left with yet another piece of fine fabric that looked like something from my dad's closet. That and a growing sense that labels really did matter: Armani, Gucci, Versace. To be revered as sacred relics, our Holy Trinity.

Am I only repeating the compulsion now? Am I still seeking, in Freudian terms, the mothering I never got, through the proxy that was the closest to—a trip to the thrift store? Am I trying to "keep her close," as my analyst might say, the way monkeys cling to their terry-cloth mothers in the wire monkey experiments, foregoing even food for the safety of secure attachment? In my defense, the thrift store and the estate sale are importantly different. One is a glorified bargain bin; the other, a bonafide portrait of a life. On my mother's desk sits a paperweight with the following quote from Oscar Wilde (and my namesake): "I have the simplest tastes: I am always satisfied with the best." The axiom is inscribed in gold. This man on Decatur has, if nothing else, rather *un*simple taste. But Freud would also say that whether you're going against them or going along with them, you're still very much doing it for *them*—your parents, whose Oedipal drama plays on.

The Quarter was fine for a jaunt that Sunday morning. When most people think of the French Quarter, they probably picture girls flashing their stuff for Mardi Gras beads and drunk tourists clutching Hand Grenades stumbling into various dens of iniquity. Not so in late winter. If *Streetcar* made the place famous for its sweltering sinful haze in the height of summer, this time of year it's more pleasant sweater weather. We donned sweaters. We parked nearby and strolled down Decatur on the sunny side of the street, holding hands. Passing Santos Bar, I was reminded, rather than of some night of depravity, of the Tuareg band we'd seen there recently. The wedding band from Niger,

Etran de L'Aïr, had transported us with their wall-of-sound guitar, and at the end of the show, the four men in desert garb put their hands together in prayer. I had felt the experience to be spiritual. Now the house was next door to Santos, which felt auspicious.

In "Street Haunting: A London Adventure," Virginia Woolf asks if it's not so much the streets you haunt, but rather the streets that haunt you. She goes off in search of a pencil ("No one perhaps has ever felt passionately towards a lead pencil," that immortal opening line). Along the way, she gets flooded with madeleine moments, the darkening London streets allowing her mind to project all kinds of fantasies. As her imagination plays out, transporting her from this cold, snow-swept winter night to a bright memory of summer ("on a balcony, wearing pearls in June"), she wonders, "Am I here, or am I there?" The art of the flaneur seems to be precisely this openness to the unexpected, the errand only an excuse to be confronted by the city streets—and your own unconscious. Like an estate sale, perhaps, the used bookstore she ends up in allows for the mystery of chance encounter, for "in this random miscellaneous company we may rub against some complete stranger."

The sign for the estate sale, as advertised, pointed us down the uneven cobblestone alley. Under the pink stone archway, we passed as if through a portal, emerging onto a courtyard of a different time and place. Stone sculptures chipped and well-weathered in the sun were scattered about the yard, and stone fountains gently trickled. The garden walls were high and enclosing; it struck me that this little piece of rustic paradise, this so very Rohmerian, private hideaway from the dizzying nightlife, would likely go for over a million today but must've been acquired for a tenth of that originally. Such was the mixed attraction of a French Quarter estate sale, flocking to the major tourist destination like anyone else with out-of-state plates but actually there to experience the neighborhood in the days before the boom, the house a kind of time capsule. Climbing the back steps, I felt the old wood giving a little underfoot, and instinctively I reached for the rickety railing, which inspired little confidence. Old shelves were crammed full of rusty tins and garden tools, and I wasn't sure whether they were for sale or part of a living museum.

Then we were standing inside the room from the photo, my fantasy—exposed beams, French doors, Persian rugs, brick hearth. My girlfriend pointed out the original cypress floors, recognizing their wide planks, and I found myself crossing them as if drawn by some invisible force. I arrived at the miniature dollhouse against the wall. Peering inside, I noticed the contents had been neatly organized by category—furniture, kitchen supplies, people. I poked around for a couch, in homage to Freud and my chosen profession, but no luck. I half-wondered if this was how my mother had seen our house, something like a lifesize dollhouse, to be systematically inventoried, stylized with interchangeable pieces, significant only insofar as they cohere and *complete the look.* I felt a sudden pang of sadness that I'd been nothing but a doll to her. (No wonder I have so much trouble dressing myself in the morning.) Then I turned and saw Ferrigno, his biceps even bigger, oilier. He was looking at me as much as I was at him. It felt carnal. This was not my mother's house.

One of the things no one tells you about estate sales is just how much of your own stuff you might encounter between the walls. Something about being in a home—any home—activates the archetype, and all the longings and fears that come with a place of origin get triggered. After swallowing my solemn mood at the dollhouse, I wandered over to a table where a set of ornate Japanese boxes caught my eye. I picked up one of them and out came tumbling a beautiful silk print of a Zen monastery with its swirling rock garden. I thought of my semester abroad in Kyoto, and the memories, so dream-like now, of the smell of incense burning in the morning and the guttural sound of chanting monks and the blue-black of the temple before dawn. I was in crisis about my life but so what? We were all in crisis, hence studying Buddhism, as Westerners are wont to do going through their "seeker" phase. Besides, we were really living someplace, intimate with it, running damp cloths along the hardwood floors so as not to allow a speck of dust to accrue. There's a Zen koan about a master who holds a poetry contest to choose his successor. One submission takes the mind to be a mirror, requiring daily wiping to keep clean, perhaps by way of meditation's purification. But it loses out, ultimately, to the one asking,

"Where can any dust alight?"

For those of us without a home to begin with, I suppose, it's easier to feel at home anywhere. This house showed evidence of a life on the move, and I wondered whether its owner felt truly at home at every new destination or only upon returning to Decatur with all the worldly memorabilia. It was like you could spin a globe and land somewhere foreign, just crossing his living room. The loft was apparently where he kept all the strictly paper ephemera, catalogued by country, filling banker's boxes with receipts and ticket stubs and pamphlets. He was definitely musically inclined, as the organ, in particular, made for a recurring motif through this kind of text. Whatever happened to his organ on a trip to Sweden, he left with the local repair shop's business card.

At some point, I saw the baton, lying there on the mantle. It seemed innocent enough, just a stick, yet somehow dignified. Other objects—a vintage pewter bell from a German

Christmas market, a Rex Mardi Gras dubloon from the 70s—were what they were, exactly that. But somehow, this wasn't what it was, or was what it wasn't, a living contradiction: powerful enough to swell the strings of an orchestra, moving us to tears, and now silent. I was afraid to reach out and touch it, the way grabbing a gun is already to take aim and holding a knife to imply cutting. ("One holds the knife," as Richard Selzer reminds us of his art of surgery, "as one holds the bow of a cello or a tulip—by the stem.") I picked it up, holding it by the darkwood handle, and just then a woman walking by smiled at me, as if anticipating the symphony to follow. Suddenly, I felt helplessly omnipotent, as if there were no way to hold it without conducting. I didn't want the attention, but like a young wizard with his first wand, the power felt intoxicating. I won't go into the phallic implications of this, but my girlfriend approved.

Somehow, I managed to get the thing to checkout without incident. But then the woman ringing me up seemed caught off guard. "Oh!" she exclaimed. "I thought it was a giant matchstick." She took it from me and held it upside down, striking it repeatedly against an imaginary matchbox. I thought of Disney's *Fantasia*, the scene where the mops and buckets dance to Stokowski (who, I found out later, was famously a free-hand conductor). Something about objects with an ear for music, I suppose. I took it from her and paid. Turning to leave, I nearly swung into the man behind me, who piped up: "What's that?" So I decided to play along. "A baton," I said, waving it around in the air faux-conductorly. "Can't you hear the music?" He smiled and said that he could.

Later that night, wondering how to sell this thing on eBay, I consulted with a friend in the art business. He works for a high-end gallery in London and has become an expert on the resale value of rare Picassos. We were on our way to Tet Fest, the Vietnamese celebration of the Lunar New Year, and it just so happened that my girlfriend and her childhood friend (of "gentle crumble" fame) were along for the ride. We were all eager to get hopped up on Vietnamese iced coffee and throw some money down on "shrimp" or "crawfish" at the bingo-like game in the gambling tent, where the old chain-smoking Vietnamese man wearing lots of gold rings and necklaces yells raspy words of encouragement into the mic. There was a palpable charge of anticipatory excitement in the air for turning a profit in our soon-to-be-caffeine-addled state when he said that, at least in his world, only one thing really mattered with used goods. Provenance.

In this case, I wish I knew. Unfortunately, I can't tell you how many times this baton has changed hands, if ever, the way he could something from an Old Master. But I can tell you that Frederick Lee Lawson (1937-2025), its former owner, was a high school math teacher much-beloved, as well as a retired naval officer. Driving to Mary Queen of Vietnam Church, out past New Orleans East, we allowed our minds to wander, imagining this baton conducting formal naval ceremonies, at least pointing at the blackboard of Algebra II. (Mr. Lawson's "incessant, somewhat impatient and exasperated tapping of his ring on lacquered desks and boards," one former student wrote on his tribute wall, "still resonates.") But we didn't have much else to go off of. In a fit of desperation, I texted another friend, a flutist who went to Juilliard and sometimes plays with the Louisiana Philharmonic, asking if he could tell from the photo anything of this baton's history. But I never heard back.

That leaves us with the history of the baton, period. French for "staff," the baton originated as exactly that, a scepter-like instrument that goes back to Ancient Greece. For

Pherekydes of Patrae, known as the "Giver of Rhythm," it was golden and used to bring lyre and Pan flute in sync. For Jean-Baptise Lully, a highly sought-after conductor in the French royal court, it was apparently fatal: while conducting *Te Deum* for King Louis XIV, missing the floor with his *bâton de direction* and instead striking his own foot, leading to gangrene and his eventual death two months later. It was around this time that the baton as we now know it started appearing in concert, perhaps on the heels of Rousseau's devastating remark about French opera conductors beating time like a "woodcutter felling a tree." Not to mention at least one crystal chandelier raining glass on the overzealous conductor whose stick-banging got a little out of control.

But for all this illustrious history, I'm tempted to call it a rather silent instrument, another of my girlfriend's coinages. As conductor Diane Wittry puts it, a conductor "makes no sound," and yet remains "responsible for the quality of the music-making." And isn't that wonderful? Magical, even—this skinny, 15-inch piece of birch, weighing barely an ounce, assuming control over dozens, if not hundreds of highly-trained musicians, swelling our hearts and bringing us all to tears? It's just a little stick, yet it marks the evolution of orchestras over the centuries, growing in size and complexity so as to require a simple solution to their leadership. If the purpose of art is defamiliarization, as theorist Viktor Shklovsky put it, "to make the stone *stony*," then I hope my little adventure with the baton makes us do a double take. I, for one, doubt I'll ever look at one the same way again.

Tufts College
19
57

Tufts College Tankard by Josh Russell

Every now and then I break a glass to make my wife feel better. I do it when she breaks a glass, which used to happen only now and then, but recently the sound of a tulip or goblet smashing on the kitchen floor is a regular occurrence. It upsets her when she does it, and I worry, vaguely, that her increasing clumsiness is because we're both getting older. We're beer drinkers. She likes dark lagers and English bitters. I prefer Belgian ales. When we first got together, thirty-three years ago, we drank High Life 40s from the Circle K down the street from her apartment. In 1993, those big bottles cost $1.99, which is how much we pay at the thrift store for replacements for the glasses we break. Books are a dollar, records are 25¢, and drinkware is $1.99, no matter if it's a dainty tasting snifter or a massive dimpled maßkrug. I could get a discount because at fifty-seven I'm considered "senior," but it makes me feel old to ask, so I pay the $1.99. A few days ago, she dropped a festbier boot from a brewery in Delaware, and I countered with a mug logoed with the name of a local bar that never reopened after lockdown. This morning, I told her I needed to go to the grocery store for a bougie frozen pizza and a case of seltzer, and she said she was going to the hardware store to get caulk. So that I wasn't lying, I stopped for the pizza and the water before I went to the thrift store to buy her a new glass. What I found for her was a ceramic tankard emblazoned with the seal of Tufts College and the date 1957. On the backside it was labeled DAVE. I knew she'd be amused by its novelty: not a pint glass from a golf course or a chain crab shack; a keepsake from a school neither of us went to; DAVE. Inside it was dusty and there was a dead fly. I took it home and scrubbed it and when she came back from True Value, I presented it to her. She hefted it, laughing, and mimed taking a big gulp of beer, then frowned and said very seriously, "I've been breaking glasses to make you feel better. I worry about how many you've dropped."

There's No Substitute for Guts: the Bear Bryant Bust, or Queer Desire in Tuscaloosa, Alabama by Katie Jean Shinkle

Do all roads of the queer heart lead back to Tuscaloosa, Alabama? This is, of course, hyperbolic and a bit rogue to say, but you must forgive my defenses. If you will go way back with me: The weeks before I left Grand Rapids, Michigan for Tuscaloosa, Alabama, I confessed my love to someone who, in the recent years prior, had finished their own tortured time of queer yearning and desire toiling over the poems that would save and demise them in Tuscaloosa. The night before I moved we kissed and I thought *that's the end* both of my Self as I knew it and anything that could manifest between us as Tuscaloosa was opening herself to me and had invited me in. Tuscaloosa represented at the time a segue into hope eternal, the hope of some kind of future Me I didn't know yet, the hope of possibility, so that I, too, could toil over the queer yearning and desire required to write the poems to save *me.* While I barreled down US-31 to I-65 to Alabama gin and appletini-hungover stomach sick heart sick brain sick so young the poetic yearning overdrive of being serious about something anything in my small adult life kicking in full force even in the face of leaving a new chapter of love behind (which *did* end up coming with me, for years, long distance, across two states, another story for another day), there was a part of me that knew Tuscaloosa was going to change the course of my life forever if I allowed it. Did I want to allow it or were the ancient gods of poetry I worshipped even at such a young age going to strike their blows anyway regardless of my desire, defiance, consent (one could only be so lucky)?

If we can cut to years later, I'm still in Tuscaloosa, heart sick stomach sick brain sick over queer desire again. A pop-up yard sale on the corner of Queen City Avenue and Alaca Place, a house full of meth-head tweakers begins at 6:00AM, their humongous dalmatians on thick chains in the front yard, sad and scared and howling at the fold-out tables filled with tchotchkes and knick-knacks and piles of stained clothing and half-broken toys and cheap Wal-Mart lamps that no longer function. They make honest work of this yard sale set-up for an entire week, rising before the sun, the dalmatians crowing on cue and digging a sinkhole. As I walked to campus and back to the neighborhood every day, the woman of the house would stare me down, her eyes huge black round things full of pleading to stop and look at her sad peddled wares. Truth be told, I didn't stop because I had no cash as this was not the time of money applications on cell phones and one should have cash for a yard sale. By Friday, however, I had convinced Laurence to go with me and I had also convinced him to lend me some dollars since he always had cash on hand like a reasonable adult. We ventured early before heading out to Indian buffet lunch to settle our hungover stomachs from the night before at the gay bar.

The woman with the huge black round things in her face for eyes was wrapped in a mint green terry cloth robe with large faded yellow flowers on it that almost looked hard it was so used and her blonde hair was matted onto the back of her head having not seen a brush or comb in a long while. I remember how beautiful she was in the morning light sitting on her porch gripping a huge coffee mug jittering on her lap and picking at her face. There was something about her high cheek bones, which were drooped and sunken in from long term drug use that glittered against the sunrise. As we perused the tables, she tried to talk to us about the various items and Laurence, ever the generous spirit, engaged in light laughter and questions but I did not, ever the glowering scowl I kept those days. There was nothing of interest to purchase and the woman could sense it, she was getting nervous because Laurence used to wear Prada eyeglass frames so she thought he probably had money and would spend it and even commented about liking his glasses which everyone did because they were very expensive and looked gorgeous on him. In one exchanged look across the tables we both knew it was time to leave, and as we were trying to go the woman was explaining some item Lau-

rence had been looking at in an attempt to convince of him of value and worth (unsuccessfully), I saw tucked away in a molding and empty box that seemed to have become a chew toy situation for the dalmatians a plaster bust of Paul "Bear" Bryant, the esteemed football coach of University of Alabama football (1958-1982) who led the Crimson Tide to six national championships.
I grabbed the bust and held it up, interrupting the woman mid-grift: "How much is this?" " O h you can just have it, I was going to throw it away," she said.

For some reason, that ended all conversation, for which I think Laurence was relieved, and we walked home in silence me clutching the Bear Bryant bust in my hands for dear life as I was shaking and in desperate need of a cocktail and some biryani.

The Bear Bryant bust, made of cheap pottery plaster, was hand painted with a bright copper metallic paint reminiscent of a bronze statue. He has his signature houndstooth fedora on his head, which one can only recognize as houndstooth through the textured, jagged, two-toned checked pattern of the mold since it is not black and white. The face chosen as the replica is one that is easily recognizable for any historic Alabama fan—a wizened look of knowing, a small genuine smile of a champion, the soft jowled cheeks of a man who understood the worth and capacity of those around him and, through hard work, dedication, grit, and discipline, pushed everyone to greatness. Or that's the lore around Paul Bryant, anyway. What we all want to believe. That's the thing about lore, and belief, and perception: So often, once established, we cannot escape its wrath.

Since I acquired this bust, it has accompanied me throughout the next 15 years of my life, through cross-country moves, new work desks and colleagues, through friendships gone and returned, through injury and illness, through death and rebirth. It has sat in boxes and been shipped through the USPS, it has been on trucks and in moving pods, it has been in backpacks and messenger bags and hanging on the wall next to my nightstand for various inspirations. It survived a house fire, COVID-19, and two devastating, life-changing break-ups which included love from Tuscaloosa. The wear and tear on it are minimal for all that movement. You can see there is a small V-shaped crack at the base of Bear Bryant's shirt collar (bottom) and there is a bit of chipped paint on the brim of his hat. But overall, the bust, like the man and legend himself, like love, remains mysterious, solid, reliable, and, against all odds, still here.

Today, I am thinking about surrogate endings or paths of divergence that lead back to Tuscaloosa for me nearly 20 years later. A queer desire and yearning, the same heart sick brain sick feelings of the pull of the ancient gods of poetry, though I am older now and understand more about the chambers of the heart-mind and its frailty and duality and suffering. I am pulled back there by meaning making, by confession, by fated circumstance which seems almost immutable in impossibility, and it probably is, as far as unrequited queer longing often goes, which is to say, nowhere. All these years later why am I confessing my love again with Tuscaloosa as a background, the complexities now so much deeper than 20 years ago when I was drunk dumb in love and only recently at the poetry altar call. What did I know then that I can let porously seep through into today? How it all blends together anyway, all this time, all this love, all this desire. It is seemingly a slow burn (is queer longing ever a slow burn?) and at times I feel fated to be alone forever even in the presences of it because love never feels quite how you wish it would and it is easy to fill the space with fantasy and hope, filled with holes and flimsy, or it comes with the price of disappointing and hurting those who continue to want you to be someone you are not. I find myself unmoored by the sheer amount of all that continues to beg us for love in this life. How can we be of service to any of it? I will, ultimately, turn my back and walk the other direction once again. But, until then, as Bear Bryant eloquently once said: There's no substitute for guts.

ORIGINAL FLAVOR
Retro Pack from the 1970's
POP ROCKS®
Crackling Candy
ORIGINAL
CHERRY
ARTIFICIALLY FLAVORED
Still Popping After 40 Years
NET WT. 0.33 OZ. (9.5G)

Still Popping After 40 Years (Pop Rocks) by Margo Steines

*Author's note: This is not *technically* a used item, because your girl has not yet mastered the art of reading the instructions before doing the assignment. That said, I'm arguing that Pop Rocks are, by definition, used, because they are a throwback to and an artifact of a time that is most definitely used: the 1980s. First released in the mid 1970s, then briefly discontinued in the mid-eighties (after the thing I'm about to tell you about) before being relicensed and reintroduced to market, Pop Rocks have always been giving used, even when they were new.*

Before the internet, we had urban legends. One of the more persistent ones in the era of my youth—the eighties—was about Pop Rocks, and it went like so: if you drink Coca-Cola and eat Pop Rocks contemporaneously, your stomach will explode. This, I realize, sounds stupid, but we a) were children, b) did not have the internet to fact check anything and c) also believed that there was LSD and/or razor blades in Halloween candy, that there were HIV-infected needles in the coin return slots of payphones, and that if you played certain records backwards they would somehow make you go psychotic.

There was a different relationship to truth and rumor back then. I got all my information from Z100, Hot97, and shit I heard on the subway and from other kids, who were getting their information the same way. Rumor and conjecture were the currencies of the day, and as Manhattan kids (the boroughs remained remarkably siloed back then), we were both sophisticated and worldly, because New York City; and also dumbasses, because kids; and also annoying, because we were dumbasses who thought we were sophisticated and worldly.

I have always had a compulsion to find out—what I'm finding, I've never really known, but if you tell me something like Pop Rocks and Coca-Cola will make your stomach explode or If you do heroin once you'll become a junkie, well, imma try some Pop Rocks and Coca-Cola, and also some heroin. That's how I know that Pop Rocks and Coca-Cola actually just give you a minorly rumbly tummy feeling, plus the gross queasy feeling of having consumed 5x your RDA of glucose. That's also how I became a junkie.

I started doing heroin in what was arguably the best era to be an intravenous drug user: after we knew better than to share needles but before everything was adulterated with fentanyl. Shooting drugs, especially if you are a dumbass, is of course a dangerous game, and I was protected as much by my generationality than by my other myriad privileges.

Once I caught a habit—which was immediately (see: dumbass)—my two biggest issues as a junkie were manifesting money and finding a place to cop. It would seem like in New York City, especially as a local, finding drugs on the street should not have been hard, but I struggled. I knew how to get every other kind of drug delivered to my house via telephone call, how to buy bad weed and really bad cocaine/baby laxative on the street, how to buy Ecstasy (that's what we used to call MDMA, kids) and ketamine at the club, and how to buy crystal meth at the gay men's bathhouses (where my presence was tersely tolerated in the lobby only), but heroin eluded me. At the time it was marked, along with crack cocaine, by a particular stigma that ran along both race and class lines, which in New York meant that it ran by neighborhood lines, and I didn't know my way around the Bronx.

I would wander around Alphabet City and the east side of Bushwick, which are now the sites of $million+ condos and the DJs whose parents buy them for them, but which at the time were giving Spike Lee, and just kind of…look around. I didn't have any friends who used dope, and even the people I smoked crystal meth with looked scandalized if I mentioned it. I once tried to cop on Lexington and 125th street after listening to Lou Reed, but there wasn't a spot there anymore, there was a Duane Reade. Sometimes I would meet someone who would help me cop, occasionally I would meet someone who would steal my cash, and once in a great while I would locate one of the roving trap houses (we didn't call them that then, we just called them "the spot," as in "the spot is closed for Thanksgiving," and yes it always was) and actually be able to transact directly on my own.

To be dependent on drugs is a nightmare and not at all a joke, but I am grateful to say that my active addiction is far enough in the rearview that I can see the irony, and perhaps even the humor, in being dependent on both the drug I had to take to avoid becoming grievously sick every six or so hours, and also being dependent on the availability and benevolence of equally addicted strangers in order to get what I needed. I was, by all accounts, an absolute failure of a junkie, and that is one of the other reasons I am alive today to write this essay and make my little jokes.

Pop Rocks were pulled off the market in the mid-eighties, when I was so young that the story itself was apocryphal by the time it reached me some years later. In order to retain the hazy veil of eighties consciousness, I resisted researching or fact checking any of this, so here's what I think I know: someone started the rumor that drinking a Coke and eating Pop Rocks made a kid's stomach explode. It went viral, in the way that things went viral back then: by word of mouth and on radio shows. Despite the dubious truth of this event, the urban legend gained so much traction that kids actually stopped eating Pop Rocks, parents forbade them, and schools including mine banned them. Eventually, under the pressure of what spiraled into an organically generated smear campaign, Pop Rocks went under and off the market. For a time, you could not find them in the bodega, which was not that big a deal because Pop Rocks, if you subtract for novelty, are honestly pretty gross.

And me? Well, I haven't eaten Pop Rocks since the time I tried them to see if my stomach would explode (it didn't). Now I'm 43, and I have IBS, so I worry about my stomach exploding for arguably less sexy reasons. I don't shoot heroin anymore, either, but I like to think I'm Still Popping After 40 Years.

The • Golden • Jubilee • Of • Her • Majesty

Queen Elizabeth II Jubilee Teacup by Gabi Stone

I saw the Queen Elizabeth teacup more than I saw my own mother.

Every day, before leaving for work at 5 am sharp, she would creep into my room, black high heels silent on the gray carpet, and leave a cup of steaming English breakfast tea with two cubes of sugar on the matching saucer. I always woke up when she came in, no matter how quiet she was, but she still crept around as if it would make a difference.

When I inevitably rolled over with a groan of drowsiness, she would lean down and plant a kiss on my forehead.

"Two sugars for the sweetest girl in the world," she would whisper before slipping out of my bedroom and into the real world.

Soon after my 10th birthday, she tasked me with cooking my own breakfast, but she never failed to leave me tea. Even the morning after Grandma died and the day she caught her boyfriend cheating, Queen Elizabeth II appeared at my bedside with her inscrutable, benevolent smile. Every morning, I would drop the sugar cubes in the steaming liquid and take a long, blissful sip under the watch of either young or old Elizabeth, depending on which side of the cup was facing me.

Mom never splurged on anything, with two exceptions: my clothes and tea. She painstakingly imported fancy, fragrant metal tins of tea from England, even during months where money was tight, which was every month. She worked twice as hard to be taken half as seriously as her male coworkers, carving lines of stress down her face. Those lines softened when she saw the weathered white box of tea on our doorstep or watched me adorn myself with a new hot pink T-shirt and jeans.

I didn't notice these things until I was older, of course. As a kid, I thought it was normal to have just one parent, a mom who worked from 6 am to 7 pm. I got used to being the last one to get picked up from daycare. Between drawing and whatever book I could get my hands on, my childhood passed quickly into the oblivion of memory.

Then Mom was laid off from her job a few months before my freshman year of high school—something about her office closing—and she wandered around with red-rimmed eyes for days. When she heard word of an open job from an old friend in Arizona, we left without looking back. We lived out of boxes for weeks in an apartment twice as big and half as expensive as our old one. I even had my own bathroom with more counter space than a single person could possibly need. I understood that this was supposed to be an upgrade, but it felt so empty without Mom's makeup strewn across every inch of counter space. If all of humanity vanished and the only evidence of our existence was this bathroom, no one would know that Mom had ever lived, and that was unfathomable.

We finally finished unpacking everything just a few days before my first day of school, but one thing was missing. I searched high and low for the teacup to no avail, though there was only one place it could have been: the medium cardboard box containing my most precious belongings, wrapped in paper and wedged between my stuffed animals and Nintendo DS. It might as well have disappeared out of thin air.

After I confessed the truth to Mom in an explosion of tears and snot, her movements became dull, like a blade in need of sharpening. My first day of school came and went in a blur of color and tears. Mom stopped making me tea, so I made it for myself every morning in a plain white mug. It tasted flat and dull, though it was the same tea as always. I missed when tea tasted like comfort, but most of all, I missed Mom. Her paychecks got bigger and my clothes got nicer, but that didn't stop her from crying behind closed doors when she thought I was asleep.

I came home from school one mild autumn day to find all of our tins of tea upturned on the counter, the leaves scattered across the marble counter and on the floor. Earl Grey, English Breakfast, and the nasty peppermint tea Mom tried to make me drink after every meal for digestive purposes littered the floor. She wasn't home yet, so I swept it all into the trash, unsure if doing so would make her feel better or worse. But there was nothing else I could do. It was my fault that the teacup disappeared, after all, even if I didn't know when or how it happened.

Two more weeks passed in uneasy silence. We skirted the spilled tea incident like a sinkhole. On a Friday night, I finally mustered the courage to talk to Mom about it.

She was in the kitchen chopping potatoes and carrots for dinner, her back turned to me. Her shoulders hovered near her ears as the knife sliced through the vegetables.

"Mom?" I asked, my voice ringing hollowly between the sharp thwock of the knife.

"Yes, honey?" she said without turning around.

"Who gave it to you?"

The knife stilled, leaving behind eerie silence. Then, to my horror, her shoulders trembled, so briefly that I thought I'd imagined it.

"Was it Dad?" I ventured.

An outlandish guess, but at least it managed to fill the silence for a couple of seconds. The word "dad" tumbled awkwardly off my tongue like a foreign word.

"No." she said, her voice sharper than the knife in her hand. "He was a master at taking, but he never learned how to give." She resumed chopping, a little faster this time, each slice cutting through the air between us.

"I'm sorry for losing it."

Mom turned around to face me for the first time. Her eyes were puffy, and I knew she had been crying again.

"It's all right, sweetheart," she said. "It's not the first thing I've lost."

It's been ten years since I left Mom and the desert behind. We call every so often; I never initiate. She verifies that I'm alive, and I think about telling her that I'm still looking for the cup before realizing it's a terrible idea.

Dad calls on a different day each year to wish me a happy birthday. He hasn't guessed right yet, but I suppose he will eventually out of sheer luck. Truthfully, I stopped searching for the teacup when I moved to Nowhere, Nebraska, for college. I couldn't even find a kindred soul there, let alone a teacup that had vanished out of thin air. Though I graduated a few years ago, I haven't found my way out yet. It's one of those quicksand places, where every fitful kick and thrash makes it harder to escape.

On an unseasonably temperate fall day, I left work early and aimlessly drove around the two-horse town. My sky blue 2008 Toyota Camry dutifully carried me past three gas stations, four fast food restaurants, two money laundering businesses, an Ace Hardware, a Dollar General, a no-name grocery store, the city hall, and a cemetery. On the edge of town, just past the cemetery, was a secondhand store. The pickings were about as good as you'd expect from a town like this, but the weather was too pleasant to go back to my apartment.

A speaker blasted the opening notes of Beethoven's Symphony No. 5 as I opened the door.

Three other people shuffled between aisles stuffed to the brim with discarded goods. I wondered what they were looking for. I wondered why I had even wandered in here in the first place.

I found myself in an aisle filled with defunct kitchen appliances: cheap heart-shaped waffle makers, blenders without lids, ancient popcorn makers, and the like. As I was about to turn the corner to the dishware aisle, I heard a shuffle of fabric that heralded a human presence. Not wanting to interact with another living soul, I prepared to turn around when the sound of shattering porcelain from one aisle over pierced through the air.

"Shit!"

I stepped into the aisle and caught sight of a guy with a radioactive green mohawk holding an intact teacup and a chipped saucer.

His eyes widened as I appeared and relaxed a little after realizing that I wasn't an employee.

"The tape unstuck when I went to pick it up," Mohawk Man offered by way of explanation. There was, in fact, a pathetic string of clear tape hanging off of the teacup.

A hideous orange price sticker with "$10.99" scribbled with a fat Sharpie obscured most of the cup's design, but something about that gold trim and muted floral design poking out from under it made me pause.

"Are you buying it?" I asked.

Mohawk Man shook his head and gently placed the set on the shelf. "Nah. With my luck, it would break between here and the register."

With an even lighter touch than Mohawk Man, I picked up the teacup and peeled the sticker off. Grayish residue from the sticker marred the cup's design, but I would recognize Queen Elizabeth II anywhere.

My hands trembled. I rotated the cup. An older Elizabeth came into view, expression as enigmatic as ever.

"Woah," said Mohawk Man, sending a jolt of surprise down my spine. I had forgotten he was there.

I peered inside the cup. Were those tea stains at the bottom the very same that I had tried so hard to scrub away during my childhood, or was it merely my desperate eyes playing tricks on me? If I looked hard enough into the cup's pearlescent void, would the past reanimate itself just for me?

Mohawk Man hummed. "They'll probably give you a discount since it's technically broken now."

My feet moved to the register before I could stop myself. I mumbled something about a broken merchandise discount to the cashier and ended up outside with the teacup safely wrapped in coarse brown paper.

I climbed into my car, locked the doors, and tore the paper into shreds. The phantom scent of black tea, bitter and heady, wafted through the car, cutting through the scent of dirt that crept into every facet of life here. Past and present snapped together like a flip phone. Queen Elizabeth hadn't aged a day, and for just that moment, I didn't know when or where I was.

With the same care one would take swaddling a child, I rewrapped the cup and saucer in the paper and buckled it into the passenger's seat.

Then I reclined my seat all the way back, tucked my left leg under my right, and called Mom.

House of Eyes (Floral Picture Frame with Photo of "Grandpa Zachary" and His Grandson "William") by Layla Todd

It looked like the kind of ugly frame Aileen expected to find at the thrift store for less than a buck or sitting on her grandma's entryway table during Easter with a photograph of adolescent bespectacled Aileen inside, childhood braces glinting with camera flash. It was made of clay and heavy with the weight of the two faces framed inside. On the back of the photograph, the names 'Grandpa Zachary' and grandson 'William' were inscribed in faint pencil. How cheerful Grandpa Zachary and little William looked, the sepia tones of the photograph aging the man and making the boy appear younger. When Aileen turned the frame toward the light, the light bounced off the reflective surface of the photograph and made the faces of man and boy almost invisible, murky shapes behind the sunshine pooling in the worn creases of the photograph. An angel wearing a polka dot apron held a bouquet of textured flowers that cascaded down and choked the frame. The flowers and leaves were hand-painted with careless strokes in pale Easter colors. Blue, yellow, pink. Straight from a do-it-yourself painting kit with half a dozen little pots of paint all held together by interlocking plastic. The angel smiled and smiled until her smile seemed to split her face like a Raggedy Ann doll.

Aileen had found the photograph in Lady Smith's old house next door not long after she moved up the mountain into the Fritz house. When Aileen bought the Fritz house, her realtor told her about Lady Smith who had lived in the tumbling house her husband had built on their homestead for the past seventy-one years. He built the house big because he knew he'd breed her until every one of its thirteen rooms were filled with children. And, according to the birth records down at the county courthouse, he'd fulfilled his promise. He died before her. She wept at his funeral and went on living in the homestead as it fell to pieces around her until her youngest son built her a new home with running water and electricity. He moved her off the mountain down into a swanky new townhouse reeking of paint in a suburb carved out between two gentle hills in the valley. Lady Smith hated the yellow lighting that seeped out of the kitchen lightbulbs and the smell of all that new plywood. She spent her final years trying to go home to her house with its spring box out back in the root cellar her husband had dug and her kitchen with its wood stove and oil lamps. Every morning she packed her clothes into a pillowcase and tied it to her walker before setting out along the suburb road walking with her eyes on the mountain. Every evening her son found her at whatever point she'd managed to get to and took her back to her new house with its doors that locked and its rooms identical to the house next door.

Aileen bought the Fritz house because it had abundant wall space. It was built on a little plot of grass hidden inside the forest high on the crest of the mountain where no cellular poles raised their globular heads and only telephone and electric wires swooped pole to pole between the trees. A thin strip of rocky driveway led off the backwater mountain road and threaded its way up through the forest to the house. The house was down the road from the ruins of Lady Smith's old place, which was bigger than the Fritzes' but too ramshackle to sell and grotesque under a thick matting of vines.

The Fritzes had wall space a plenty. The Fritzes were a family of eleven. There were ten Fritz gravestones on the hill overlooking the house half hidden where the trees began to overtake the grass, but Aileen couldn't see them from the house and the dead didn't bother her. She was a family of one not counting her boxes of photographs. She had run out of wall space to hang her expanding collection at her last home in the city and had sold it to buy the Fritz place at a price too good to pass up. Pennies, practically. And the ruins of Lady Smith's homestead so close by excited her.

Aileen had no pictures of herself and certainly no photos of her family. She avoided mirrors. Instead, she covered her walls in framed photographs of strangers. She bought them at Goodwill's for between one and five dollars. She picked them out of dumpsters and rescued them from yard sales. She scavenged them out of rotting houses slowly disappearing into the earth in the backwaters of the mountain. Lonely forgotten people like herself who deserved the company of each other.

Aileen played match maker with the people in her photographs, coupling the frames and assigning the couples children from the available array of pictures she had. She arranged the framed photos on her walls in little families. Sometimes the families expanded. Sometimes the people in the photographs divorced and moved to another wall. It was never their choice. Aileen controlled the lives of the people in her photographs ruthlessly, ripping families apart at the height of their happiness.

Standing in her bedroom wall with the photograph in hand, Aileen surveyed the wall above her vanity. She decided on the bedroom because she liked to keep an eye on her new possessions. Perhaps Grandpa Zachary and little William were Lady Smith's relatives. The room she'd found the photograph in might have been a nursery. The stuffed animals there were little wisps of cloth molded to the floorboards, their guts carried away by rodents and birds and their glassy button eyes staring up at the collapsing ceiling.

Aileen had several families celebrating birthdays in the frames on her wall. Little May May even had a pinata she was whacking at blindfolded with a broom handle. Little May May had no grandfather, only a single mother and a father that had moved into the living room to take up residence with a prostitute named Diva and her pitbull. May May needed a grandfather who would neglect her for the rest of her life in favor of her new half-brother left on the doorstep by Diva.

Aileen hung the photo of Grandpa Zachary and little William on the wall beside little May May and her pensive straight-faced mother. She stepped back and sat down on the edge of her bed to survey the addition of the photo to her wall. The light creeping in through the bedroom window kept catching in Grandpa Zachary's eyes. He glared at her. Her own grandfather used to glare at her when he sat her on his knee as a girl to distract from his lecherous glances at her later.

Aileen got up. She took the photograph of Grandpa Zachary and William off the wall. She held it in her hands and thought how easy it would be to snap the ugly little thing in two, to break the flowers off the frame and crumble the old clay in her palms, to separate Grandpa Zachary from little William. She stared down at the photograph until the gleaming light bouncing off little Willam's face forced hot tears out of her eyes.

She hung the frame back up with photograph facing the wall.

Bud Vase by Jae Towle Vieira

I thought giving birth would be a worldly experience, you know, blood and torn muscle, some sleep deprivation, some fear. I figured whatever pain would come along with the contractions would be familiar, probably just like menstrual cramps but more intense. I didn't realize I was making an assumption when I assumed that all of the sensations involved would be extensions of things I had already felt, feelings that could be mapped onto a preexisting chart.

And then I lived through the birth and in the living I realized that I was wrong. As the contractions got worse, I fell into a kind of trance, and the trance began to dampen all the noise in my brain. You know, just the nonessential stuff at first: my capacity for analysis, my ability to make clear memories, the power of speech. But somehow the haze didn't dampen the pain. It was more like I was reduced to a sliver of myself, like a melting ice cube, and the waves of pain wore me down, but I could never disappear. I could only get smaller and smaller and smaller. In the end, to get my baby out and to get myself out, I had to claw.

On the other side, I had a baby to care for—a little miracle, a tiny wonder, a morning glory who got bigger and bigger and bigger—except now I had to live in a body and mind that had proven themselves to be beyond my understanding.

I gave away all my clothes and most of my stuff. I kept my colored pencils, my sketchbook, my chapstick, and this vase. They can stay for just a while longer.

The colored pencils and the sketchbook go together: the pencils get smaller and the pages fill with drawings. The chapstick has been with me for a long time. I would like to get down to empty plastic. Maybe I'll even wash out the case when it's done, so that you won't be able to tell that the balm used to smell like roses.

The vase is just a little thing. It's pleasant to hold, smooth and yet rough, light and yet heavy enough to do the job, whatever the job may be. It was sculpted carefully, by hand: a peeling of the clay along eight paths, and then eight smaller paths, and then eight smaller paths. The channels are uneven, as is the silhouette. Someone had to hold steady to make this little thing. Someone knew this vase would become itself in the paring.

The Last Thing She Gave Me (Bottle w/ Unknown Powder) by Natalia Williams

I honestly didn't think much of it when Freya gave it to me. She said, "This is the stuff of dreams."

It was just an ordinary bottle. There was nothing seemingly special about it, really. It was small, weighing less than a pound, slightly taller than my middle finger, with a stripped smooth wooden cap that resembled the bottom of an acorn. It didn't fit perfectly, so a tiny bit of its contents would leak if you turned it too much, or in my case, chucked it. It was shaped sort of like a gourd, or I guess more like a potion bottle if you're more whimsical. A third of the bottle was filled with a finely grained, pinkish-brown powder that sort of shimmered like crushed eyeshadow. By all means, though, it was an ordinary glass bottle.

I, of course, replied to her statement with, "Yeah, right. Is that why the powder has a pink hue to it?"

"Of course, silly." Freya said it as if it were the most obvious thing.

I honestly don't know how she said that sort of thing with a straight face. But that was who Freya was.

It was the way that she looked at it that probably made me keep it close. Freya would just stare at it, marveling at the way the powder shifted and moved, revealing bits of white shards. She set it down on our bedside table. The orange pill bottles, illuminated by the lamp, casted an orange glow on the little bottle. For some reason, I thought it was wrong for it to sit there, so I moved it to our dresser. But then the white bits caught my attention. I had never noticed them before.

"If the powder is the stuff of dreams, what are those little white fragments?" I asked.

"They are the bits of fallen stars that crashed to Earth in order to grant our wishes." She answered quickly as if she was certain of that fact alone.

"Careful, the poet in you is showing."

Freya playfully whacked my arm. "You love my poetic self."

She was not wrong, but I wasn't going to admit that. Not right now. But where she thought bits of fallen stars, I thought crushed bones. As you can see, we were totally in sync.

One morning, as Freya was fidgeting with the bottle, I finally asked the question weighing on my mind. "Why'd you give this to me if you liked it so much? I mean, you look at it more than I do."

"You need more whimsy. Less crushed bones."

Out of all the things I thought she was going to say, that wasn't on my list. I was expecting some nonsense like, "because you needed it," or "because you're sad and need some hope." I guess I was expecting something more sappy. Although, I wasn't too far off.

"I am perfectly whimsiful."

"It's whimsical," she said matter-of-factly. "And the word you're looking for is demonic."

"Me? Demonic? I am the most whimsiful person you know."

The look on her face said, 'What am I going to do with you?' She just shook and threw her head back, laughing dryly up at the ceiling. But then those laughs turned to coughs. Freya quickly held her hand up to stop me from rushing to her.

"I'm fine! Just choked on air," she said, giving me a small grin, before doing a little twirl. "See, your darkness is going to kill me!"

"I'm an angelic being! I don't know what you're talking about," I said, turning my head to the side indignantly.

Maybe I was demonic, maybe the bottle was the stuff of dreams. Maybe it was just a bottle. Maybe it was the stuff of nightmares.

The bottle really didn't have anything to do with it, but nevertheless, when my little world came crashing down, I blamed it: If you're really the stuff of dreams and wishes and all that stupid stuff, please, please, please make her better.

I watched her decay more and more, her figure shrinking in on itself.

"I really think you should go to the hospital, Freya."

"It's not that ba—" She was cut off by another coughing fit.

I prayed on that stupid bottle, but nothing changed. It did nothing. Well, maybe not nothing. I might've been crazy, but it felt heavier in my hands than it used to and looked to be fuller. I shook off those thoughts.

Freya was disappearing. I had nothing else to blame but the crushed bone shards in the little bottle. By the time I finally convinced her to go to the hospital, it was too late.

Then she flatlined. That single extended beep echoed in my head. I'm not sure how or when I got home that night. All I know is that I chucked the little bottle with all my might. I regretted it immediately, but it flew through the air, bits of powder flinging out as it hit the back of the couch and fell on a cushion before rolling off onto the soft rug, landing upright. That both made me want to destroy it and keep it safe.

I sat there, my back against the door, staring at the little bottle.

"Why didn't you answer my wish? Fulfill my dreams? She was…"

I don't know how long I sat there. I was feeling everything and nothing. Part of me was still staring blankly at the heart monitor as doctors and nurses shouted different things, trying to shock her back to life. But she was already gone. I knew it. They knew it.

"You were in so much pain. I don't blame you for leaving. Okay, that might be a lie."

I took to talking to the air like Freya could hear it. If I weren't doing that, I would scream at the stupid little bottle, confessing cries of anger or questioning it. Things like:

"Why'd you take her?" and "Don't leave me here alone!"

I would drive myself crazy with the what-ifs. I played it over and over, the day she first got sick. Better yet, when she first got prescribed the meds. Part of me thinks I could change the outcome if

I went back, but the other part knows this outcome was inevitable. I mean, who am I, and the little bottle, against death?

Then one day I stared at the bottle. Like, really stared at it. I wasn't going crazy. There was more pinkish-brown powder in it. I lifted the small bottle to examine it, but my hands began to shake under its weight.

My first thought was, "Do you thrive on my pain?"

I know that's irrational, but I mean, look, I was in a dark place, okay.

After a bit of calm reflection (screaming at the bottle), I tried to put that thought aside and think like her.

I don't know how to be whimsical, but perhaps it was storing my pain, so that I didn't have to carry it all. At least, that is what I'd like to think. Perhaps Freya knew she was going to die, and that's really why she gave me the little bottle.

It was probably a coincidence, but after it got quite full, I was sleeping easier. It was most likely because some time had passed. But I didn't care.

Then, I left. I left our apartment full of so much joy and pain. The laughs crashing into the sobs, the smiles catching the tears. I had to let go.

After all my things were cleared from the apartment, I set the little bottle on a little nightstand-type table in the middle of the living room.

The bottle was full. It did all that it could for me, and it was too heavy for me to take with.

Goodbye, little bottle.

I fill this bottle full of secrets.
Misplaced hearts, things I've kept that cut the deepest.
Little scars that make me sleepless.
I close my eyes, and

I gently pulled the door shut, softly locking it with a quiet click, and when I walked away, I did not look back.

HIP
HOP

Hip Hop Harry by Sierra Ziemann

This Harry, one of many manufactured, has lived for twenty-four years. He is unique in many ways. With ears that are pristinely white, hardly any dust on him, and his yellow long sleeved shirt morphing into baggy blue jeans, he doesn't seem to age. His red cap on backwards and "hip hop" declared on his shirt, makes him one of the children. He still hops to his hip tunes, a jolting unnatural hop, but endearing none the less. He once lived on a dresser and held that same smile, hopefully turned up with black beads for eyes that seemed alive.

I often waited for him to come alive in my childhood bedroom, sitting on the floor chanting, "You can do it Harry. Move! Speak!" He seemed seconds away from animating, waving his little arms at me, or hopping away from his stagnant post. Of course, nothing ever happened until I pressed the button on his hand.

I had gotten him good as new, tore his box up which I regret now, and had played every day with him for months. Despite his soft face and arms, the rest of his body was plastic and hard. I kept trying to make him dance, but without pressing his button, he really didn't do that much.

Still, I had that obsession that every child easily manifests and played out all kinds of stories I could never recall now. Harry complied, what else could he do?

But then I lost him. One night, I had snuck out of bed to play with him, anxious for a distraction from the yelling downstairs. I had sat there with watery eyes, staring close to his face, and I whispered what I had always wished for, a friend. I fell asleep while holding him, curled up on the carpet.

The next day I couldn't find him anywhere, not under the bed, in the closet, anywhere in the house. I cried for that silly dancing rabbit, and my parents scrambled to find him, but nothing.

A day later, there was knocking on the front door, and my mom called me downstairs.

"This is our new neighbor honey, his name is Robby, he wanted to see if you want to play." I hid shyly behind my mother's leg, still in a mood about Harry, but I peeked out to look at him. He looked familiar, but I knew I didn't know him. He had dark eyes and pale skin but looked sort of goofy with his lanky limbs and baggy clothes. Still, he wore a big smile, and I could see his two front teeth were quite big.

My mother eventually coaxed me into going outside with him, I found him quite intriguing anyway. It turned out to be a lot of fun, though we didn't talk much, but we played tag for hours.

Robby coming over that summer became an almost daily ritual, which was fine by me, and I quickly learned that his vocabulary was limited. I was no Hemingway at eight, but even I could say more than a few words at a time.

"Robby?" I said.

"Yes?" He looked up from our game of catch, ball in hand.

"You don't know many words do you?"

"I know words, just, still learning." He seemed a bit upset, so I comforted him.

"That's okay Robby, you're my best friend." Robby smiled at this and nodded.

The only thing was, he didn't seem to learn any more words at all. If anything, he was losing them. Over time, his phrases became one-word sentences. Being an only child, I was just happy he wanted to be my friend, but things started getting more difficult.

Robby began to get, jumpy. whenever we'd play outside, he'd start running the other way when a car drove by. When mom brought snacks, he didn't want any of the fun stuff like juice and candy. I'd find him around the corner of the house trying to eat the grass! "Mom says that isn't allowed," I'd tell him. He'd look at me with grass-stained cheeks and a blank stare.

Robby began using his blank stare quite often, in fact. Whenever I'd ask him a question or say something funny, he'd look at me confused, and then say, "Friend," with a smile. I would always nod and agree.

I was starting to get annoyed, and I was thinking of not playing with Robby anymore until one day, we were outside, and a dog started chasing us. I was running ahead but once Robby caught up to me with the dog right behind us, I was preparing to get bit, but they zoomed right past me. I stopped right there in the alley, looking dumbfounded.

The dog was fixated on Robby and bit his arm until I chased him off. Robby got stitches. I felt so bad, I couldn't stop being friends with him now.

I told mom I felt bad for him a week later, thinking of him at home confined to his bed.

"Why don't we have him over?" she suggested. I didn't really want him to, but soon enough, there he was at the door.

"Just one night," mom had said.

I wasn't happy about it, but I figured it wouldn't be very long.

Unfortunately, I was wrong.

That night we had made a little fort in the living room where we fell asleep. I woke to a thumping noise, like someone was jumping up and down on the second floor. Wondering where Robby went, I went to find the sound and make sure he was okay.

The noise led to my bedroom and as I turned the knob irrational fear rose, I wondered if something had gone horribly wrong. My heart was beating hard and I could barely work up the courage to push open the door.

What I found was Robby, on all fours, hopping around and stomping his feet.

"Robby?" He looked at me and leaned onto his back legs, with beady eyes and no sign he knew me or knew anything really. This confirmed to me my suspicions, he was somehow getting worse, and worse than I thought. As I looked at him in the dark, I noticed something as he moved.

Great long, white ears. Rabbit ears? My eyes widened, where did he get those? I went to reach out and touch them but Robby quickly turned his head, and I jumped back at the sight of his rabbit teeth and nose. He was smiling at me, and suddenly I recognized that smile and those beady black eyes. It was other things too, like his red cap and red converse.

I spoke quietly, "Harry?" It nodded slowly. "What happened to you?" My curiosity won as I touched his ears. They were warm. Not an outfit then. I poked his stomach, but I jumped back again. It was hard like plastic.

He stood slowly and began walking towards me. I fell backward when the song started playing, the one my Harry toy would always sing.

Down the trail I'm comin', with a basket full of fun
And everybody's doing the Easter hop hop hop
So put your feet together
There is nothing better
Than everybody doing the Easter hop hop hop

As he sang his song, I knew he was the same Harry I had lost but I had no time to wonder how that could be. The music was loud.

"Please stop!" I screamed as he sang loudly, stepping towards me. And every time he said hop, he would stomp his large plastic feet that would shake the floor, getting uncomfortably close to my legs.

I had to think quickly. I looked around the old room for anything to stop this nightmare, and there it was. I grabbed the bat and stood with confidence. I stared him down and swung over and over just enough to shock him as I jumped onto his back and tackled him to the ground.

Go, now you've got it! I tore open the velcro, hopeful that my plan would work. The switch was off. I swung my bat at where the plastic was screwed down, cracking it. I pulled open the heavy plastic, the corners cutting into my hands. Everything was ten time bigger, but I pried the first battery out as

Harry struggled, then the second, *Ha ho! Now you're really hoppiiingh…* then the third.

He whirred to a halt. Then he shrunk.

What was left was same old, toy Harry. Same size, same clean red cap, red shoes, yellow shirt and blue jeans.

I began to cry. I didn't want to lose Robby, or Harry, whatever his name was. He taught me what being a friend meant. My mother came running into my room, confusion on her face as she looked over the scene. She pulled me in her arms.

I never really knew why Harry came alive or became someone else, but I always held onto him. Despite what had happened, he got me through a tough time. Maybe he can do that for someone else. Over the years I've come to terms with this being just as real or as fantastical, as terrifying as any other story. I like to think Harry needed a friend as much as I did, I mean he came alive despite what would happen to him. Imaginary or not, he'll be your best friend.

Contributors of Significance

Alisa Alering is the author of the novel *Smothermoss* (Tin House, 2024), a Shirley Jackson Award Finalist that the *New York Times Book Review* calls "a compulsive journey through a wild, unknowable landscape and the wilder hearts of young girls." A former librarian and science and technology reporter, they grew up in the mountains of Pennsylvania and now live in the Sonoran Desert of Arizona.

Lofton Allen is a short story writer, essayist, and poet from Southern Arizona. His primary authorial inspirations are family dynamics, friendships, backcountry adventures, insecurities, nature, work, and love. He is currently caught up in the endless pursuit of accurately expressing how he feels, and sometimes what he thinks, through his writing. His greatest fear is being misunderstood. He has a deep love for sonoran hotdogs. He is extremely grateful to anyone who chooses to read his writing.

Brisa Bejarano found her love of writing early on in life. Her early work consists of immortalizing her cousins as sea animals, and fan fiction scribbled in lost notebooks. In recent years, you can find her writing coming-of-age while blasting EDM music. Read her work!

Sarah Blackman teaches creative writing at the Fine Arts Center, a public arts high school in Greenville, South Carolina. She is the author of *Mother Box and Other Tales* and *Hex,* and her new novel, *Nobody's Here*, is forthcoming from FC2 in the Spring of 2027. She has become very attached to Eat Bugs and is sad to see him go.

Megan Campbell lives in Tucson, AZ where she sells vintage clothing & hoards cats. Find her on bsky @meganc or on Etsy at BadChollaVintage

Adrienne Celt is the author of three novels, including *End of the World House; Invitation to a Bonfire,* which was an Indie Next Pick and named one of the best books of the summer by *O Magazine* and *Elle;* and *The Daughters,* which won the 2015 PEN Southwest Book Award for Fiction and was shortlisted for the Crawford Award. Also a cartoonist, she published a book of comics with New Michigan Press called *Apocalypse How? An Existential Bestiary.* Her work has appeared in the *O. Henry Prize Stories, The New York Times Magazine, The New Yorker, McSweeney's Quarterly Concern, Zyzzyva, The Greensboro Review, Strange Horizons, TriQuarterly,* and many other places. Since 2010 she's been publishing a webcomic at loveamongthelampreys.com.

Ryan Daniels has a Bachelor's in Studio Art and a Minor in Creative Writing at the University of Arizona. Writer for Symbol of Sailing and Memories. Combining both artistic and writing skills for future projects in a career.

Dana Diehl is the author of *The Earth Room* (Black Lawrence Press, 2026), *Our Dreams Might Align* (Splice UK, 2018) and the collaborative collection, *The Classroom* (Gold Wake Press, 2019). Her chapbook, *TV Girls,* won the 2017-2018 New Delta Review Chapbook Contest judged by Chen Chen. Diehl earned her MFA in Fiction at Arizona State University. Her work has appeared in *North American Review, Passages North, Necessary Fiction, Waxwing, Mid-American Review,* and elsewhere.

Mackenzie Dougherty is a college senior majoring in English and Creative Writing. In her free time, she writes about fantastical adventures and human experience, reads fairytales, watches horror movies, and entertains her diabolical cat, Nala. She works on publishing her short form fiction and nonfiction while pursuing a career with Universal Studios.

Paul Ducker studies history at the University of Arizona. Most of his professional studies involve the early modern period, while his personal studies revolve around ancient and classical era works, which may involve similar pieces to the one here.

Timothy Dyke is a writer and teacher who lives in Honolulu, Hawaii.

Megan Culhane Galbraith is the founder of The Writer's Collective and is the Director of the Bennington Writing Seminars. She's a connoisseur of found objects and plays with creepy dolls for her art and in service to her writing. You can find more about her here: www. megangalbraith.com

Yadira Garcia Soto is a soon-to-be graduate at the University of Arizona with a Creative Writing degree, writing a novel and suffering for anxiety.

Mahsel Gatan studies English and Creative Writing at the University of Arizona. He spends his time pacing anxiously over writing instead of spending his time writing anxiously, and the anxious pacing might show up in his writing when he does.

Valyntina Grenier is a multi-genre artist living in Eugene, Oregon. She is the author of four poetry chapbooks and one full length collection. You can find those books at Bottlecap Press, Finishing Line Press, Cathexis Northwest Press and various places where books are sold. Her recent poems and visual art have appeared or are forthcoming in *Beyond Words Magazine, Beyond Queer Words,*

Querencia, and *Wild Roof Journal*. You can find her, her visual art and links to her work around the web at valyntinagrenier.com. She is a reader for the Cathexis Northwest Press online journal and recently selected a winner for their Women of Oregon Poetry Manuscript Contest.

Avery Gregurich lives and writes in eastern Iowa, and organizes The Out Of Towners Reading Series.

Danielle Hartshorn is an English and Creative Writing student at the University of Arizona. Outside her studies, she enjoys cozying up with a cup of coffee and spending time with friends.

Wes Holtermann's writing has appeared in *The Los Angeles Review of Books*, *The Kenyon Review*, and elsewhere. He was the Hoffman Halls Emerging Artist Fellow at the University of Wisconsin in 2020. He is a gardener, living and working in Berkeley, California, and is the author of *Pleasure Herbal*, a zine series about gardening.

Caitlin Horrocks is author of the story collections *Life Among the Terranauts* and *This Is Not Your City*, both *New York Times Book Review* Editor's Choice selections. *The Wall Street Journal* named her novel *The Vexations* one of the Ten Best Books of 2019. Her stories and essays appear in *The New Yorker*, *The Best American Short Stories*, *The PEN/O. Henry Prize Stories*, and elsewhere. She lives in Grand Rapids, Michigan.

Reed Karaim, who lives in Tucson, Arizona, has written for *National Geographic*, *Smithsonian*, *Congressional Quarterly Researcher*, *Architect*, and many other publications.

Alexi L is a senior at University of Arizona majoring in Psychology and minoring in Anthropology and Creative Writing. She plans to become a published author one day while pursuing a career in counseling.

Isabel Lage is a fourth-year at the University of Arizona, double majoring in creative writing and dance. Already the most sensical person she knows, she has decided it is time to pass the Common Sense Vase along to someone else.

Jacquelyn Lo Bianco is an undergraduate student at the University of Arizona and wrote this piece with all of the late nights in mind.

Sean Lovelace lives in Indiana, where he chairs the English Department at Ball State University. He wrote *Fog Gorgeous Stag* (Publishing Genius Press), *How Some People Like Their Eggs* (Rose Metal Press), and other flash fiction collections. He has won numerous national literary awards, including the Rose Metal Press Short Short Prize and the *Crazyhorse* Prize for Fiction. And he likes condiments.

Juan Martinez is the author of the novel *Extended Stay* (2023) and the story collection *Best Worst American* (2017). He lives near Chicago and is an associate professor at Northwestern University. His work has appeared most recently in *EPOCH, Ploughshares, The Chicago Quarterly Review, The Sunday Morning Transport,* and elsewhere, and is forthcoming in *Something Followed Us Home: Tales of Latine Horror.*

Andrew Maynard purchased this Garden Angel for 3 dollars at Furbish Thrift in Richmond, Virginia, where he lives with his wife and two sons.

Porter Norton McDonald is based out of Tucson, Arizona. His art examines American identity, our relationship to the land we inhabit, consumerism, and the algaeic super-bloom of modern technology. Inspired by the cartoons and comics of his childhood, his work ranges from murals to comics to sculptural installation and has been shown in Tucson at Pidgin Palace Arts, the Lionel Rombach Gallery and the Mexican Consulate. He has performed excerpts from his current book *On Dogs on TV* at Wave Archive, Desierto Books (Tucson) and the Poetry Lounge (Pittsburgh). Porter is currently an MFA student in Illustration/Design/Animation at the University of Arizona.

Ted McLoof teaches English and Creative Writing at the University of Arizona. His work has appeared or is forthcoming in *Ninth Letter, Kenyon Review, Los Angeles Review, Hobart,* and elsewhere. His cultural criticism and book reviews can be found in *The Rumpus.* He is the author of two story collections, the latest of which, *Empty Calories and Male Curiosity,* was shortlisted for the Dzanc story prize and is available now.

Christian Moher is a writer, poet, and free-range chicken of a man who lives in Tucson, Arizona. He has many interests including medicine and mental health, fronting the new desert rock band Palo Verde Death Blossoms, spending way too much time video gaming, and trying to figure out what he wants to do when he grows up.

Eliza Moher lives in Tucson and is a recent graduate with a BA in English Literature. She is currently fighting to keep independent book stores alive and works at Antigone Books on 4th.

Ander Monson is the author of, most recently, *Predator: a Memoir, a Movie, an Obsession* (Graywolf).

Rodrigo Restrepo Montoya is the author of two novels: *Bruto* (forthcoming in 2027) and *The Holy Days of Gregorio Pasos* (Two Dollar Radio, 2023). His work has appeared in *The Kenyon Review, The Offing, DIAGRAM, Triangle House Review,* and *Joyland*. A finalist for the 2025 DAG Prize in Literature, he has an MFA in Fiction from the University of Wisconsin–Madison.

Son of a Black father and white mother, **Matthew Morris** is the author of *The Tilling* (Seneca Review Books, 2024), an essay collection that explores mixed-race identity through the trope of the "tragic mulatto." He is a graduate of the Arizona MFA program and is pursuing a PhD in English at Mizzou. Matt grew up in Virginia and believes in his home state's tag line: "Virginia is for lovers." He is always on the lookout for his next tennis buddy & pickup basketball game.

Aidan Murray is a student at the University of Arizona studying Law and Creative Writing. He will be graduating in May 2026 and begin preparing for the LSAT. He lives with his two friends and their three dogs.

David Mutschler is definitely not Dr. Divad Relhcstum. Born in Tucson, Arizona, this prolific writer and artist has worked in film, print, music, voiceover work, and advocates for neurological disease awareness. The Co-founder of Chicago-based firm ILL FAME PUBLISHING LLC, he currently resides in South Tucson with his fiancé, two sons, two cats, two miniature Doberman pinschers, two chickens and an axolotl. David is currently working on two novels, two teleplays, two podcasts, himself, two EPs, and a partridge and a pear tree. He hopes they all turn out well.

L. C. J Owen is a writer living in Tucson, Arizona.

Lydia Paar is an essayist and fiction writer. Her first full-length essay collection, *The Entrance is the Exit: Essays on Escape,* was released in 2024 from the University of Georgia Press here.

Dorian Rolston is a psychotherapist and essayist living in New Orleans, LA.

Josh Russell's most recent books are *King of the Animals* (LSU Press) and *Commonplaces* (New Michigan Press). He lives in Decatur, Georgia.

Katie Jean Shinkle says Roll Tide Roll. She teaches and writes in East Texas.

Margo Steines is the author of the critically acclaimed memoir-in-essays *Brutalities: A Love Story,* published with W.W. Norton.

Gabi Stone is a Creative Writing and French major at the University of Arizona and a participant in the English Honors program. When she's not in class, you can find her playing *Hatsune Miku: Project Diva Future Tone* on her PS4 or listening to the *Legend of Zelda: Breath of the Wild* soundtrack.

Layla Todd is studying Creative Writing at the University of Arizona. She grew up unschooled in rural Virginia and writes stories that foreground the people of the Appalachian region.

Jae Towle Vieira [they/them] is a writer and editor from northern California. They work as a producer for the podcast *Normal Gossip*. They have an MFA in Fiction from the University of Arizona.

Their fiction has been published in *The Normal School, New England Review, Carve Magazine, Passages North, Fairy Tale Review,* and elsewhere.

Natalia Williams has never seen crushed bones or killed someone. She has more important things to undertake, like completing her undergrad coursework as a junior at the University of Arizona or writing stories and poetry at 2:33 am at the top of a parking garage, in the basement of a building on campus, or in her lifeless soul-sucking cave of a room. She is a reader of fiction, enjoying romance, isekai, sci-fi, and mystery novels, as well as webcomics. When not writing or reading, she likes to take late-night drives into the middle of nowhere with her friends, where they scream into the darkness.

Sierra Ziemann is a senior majoring in creative writing and professional and technical writing at the University of Arizona. She has previously had four poems published in *SandScript* 2024 and won the third-place poetry award. She is also working with Make Way for Books on a children's book publication for their app, and most recently had a poem published for *Persona* Creative Magazine 2025. She currently reads poetry submissions for *Sonora Review.*

www.ingramcontent.com/pod-product-compliance
Lightning Source LLC
LaVergne TN
LVHW081323110826
845149LV00007B/1574

9781971740058